CRAP HOLIDAY

CRAP HOLIDAY

JENNY MORRILL

ISBN: 9781726871235

DEDICATIONS

Thank you to the following people for helping, nagging, or otherwise getting up in my business:

Dad
Alex
Simon
Jason
Glyn
Aaron

ABOUT THE AUTHOR

Jenny Morrill writes the nostalgia and pop culture blog World of Crap. Occasionally, Den of Geek will take pity on her and allow her to write for them.

She once attempted to eat 36 trios in one go, after watching Highlander while drunk one night.

1. STEVE

I once caught a man having a piss in a Pot Noodle, so this is nothing. I just tut.

Me and this guy are caught in a weird stand-off; he's refusing to pay for the chicken, I'm refusing to give him the chicken for free just because he claimed someone else looked at it. I'm starting to wish I could iron my own face off.

The man's reasoning is that because "she picked it up and she was looking at it while I was there", the chicken is now damaged goods, and he can get it for free.

"Did she do anything else to the chicken?"

I really want to say 'This woman doesn't fucking exist does she', but I control myself because I'm a useless coward. I tried to confront a shoplifter once, but he shouted hip-hop at me, and then he threw a crunchie at my head and my eye went a bit funny for half an hour. After that we got Nick, and now Nick is supposed to deal with felons and general scrota.

"I just told you, she picked it up and she was holding it and looking at it."

"And this was the only chicken left?"

"No."

"But you still chose this chicken."

"Yes. I have a right to choose this chicken, it's the one I want. And I have a right to get it for free now."

You don't realise how hideous the public are until you have to interact with them, with their weird smells and their inability to press buttons. And somehow they're all called Alan. But the worst thing by far is this insistence that they have rights. 'I have a right to a refund, I have a right to shop after you close, I have a right to let my shit-covered kid open all the crisps and drop them on the floor, it is my human right.'

This guy doesn't give a shit about his rights, he's after a free chicken. There wasn't even a woman looking at the chicken. I never saw a woman. I bet he walked right up to the shelf and chose that chicken. I bet he said to the chicken "Hey baby, it's your lucky night."

I don't need this. I didn't get any sleep last night because Joanne has decided, without my permission, to paint the living room Chemical Burn Yellow. It looks like a fucking highlighter pen.

"Ta da! What do you think?" she'd said, as if I was going to think anything other than 'I want to kill myself'.

"If you don't change it back to 'Extra Plain', or whatever the fuck it was we had before, I'm going to phone the police and tell them you don't live here and that you're a burglar. And that you've been printing pound notes."

She looked deflated. Was it possible she'd thought I was going to enjoy looking at this?

"And it stinks. Why does it stink?"

"It's vegan paint!"

"Paint isn't supposed to smell like shit Joanne."

"God, it's ethical! What, are you against the planet or something?"

"Yes I am. Very much. I hate the planet."

"Well I'm sorry but I needed to paint it this colour. For cleansing rituals. A vibrant, energetic yellow helps to harness the fire energies in the room, and they're getting really depleted."

My eyes rolled into the back of my head.

"Jesus, fire energies? I might have preferred it if you'd actually set the house on fire."

"God you're so closed minded!"

"Look, I've had a long day, we'll argue about this to-morrow. I'm going to have an early night."

She stopped me as I got to the stairs. "Oh, don't forget, I'll be lighting some lemongrass at four o'clock."

"What? In the morning?"

"I told you, remember? Four o'clock is the optimum time to harness female moon energies, because the moon is going to be aligned with Sweden..."

"In the morning?"

"Oh God you're so closed minded! The 'traditional' day–night cycle was an invention of the patriarchy to keep us awake doing cleaning and sex!"

At four o'clock the smoke alarm woke me up, and then I couldn't get back to sleep because the fumes from the fluorescent shit paint kept me awake.

Anyway, that's why I didn't get any sleep.

I want to get rid of the man. I toy with the idea of just starting to cry so he'll leave, but I can't summon the energy. Would he still want the chicken if I shoved it up his arse?

I go through my options:

1. I give the man a free chicken, and he gets a free chicken. This is not going to happen, because the cost of the chicken would come out of my wages. I do not like this man enough to give him £4.63. So I am not giving him a free chicken.

2. I sit here and argue with him until it's time to go home. That won't take too long, I think it's nearly home time. I sneak a glance at the clock. Oh, I still have another seven and a half hours.

3. I call my boss and leave her to deal with the man. I can't do this, because five minutes ago Karen announced that she was going to the toilet to do yet another pregnancy test. She'll cry if she's pregnant. She'll cry if she's not pregnant. If she has to come out to deal with a chicken, she might very well steal the chicken and dress it up like a baby and call it Jared.

4. I call our security guard to deal with the man. I look over, and Nick is sitting there reading *CROCHET GIRL!* magazine. It is a magazine for teenage girls that really love to crochet. Their only reader is Nick. I don't like to bother Nick, because for all he claims to know 'kung fu', I don't think he even knows how to cover his own bollocks in a fight.

I'm basing this on the time I asked him to apprehend some teenagers who were shaking all the cans, and he claimed he had a sudden water infection and ran into the toilet.

I guess I'm on my own. Great – I've got a fucking yellow living room that smells of shit, and this man wants a free chicken, and I can't take much more.

I'm about to yell at the man about my yellow room and call him a shaved bollock, when I have an idea. It's not necessarily a professional idea, but it's all I've got for now.

I smile at the chicken man. He responds by wiping something on his jacket.

"Yes sir, I think our policy states that you are entitled to receive this chicken at no cost to you. It's covered under the… 'immediate area and surrounding area contamination of poultry and sundries' clause in our customer satisfaction policy."

He stops wiping. I think I've caught him off guard. He wasn't expecting this to work, he wasn't really expecting to get a free chicken. I fucking knew it. He's a chicken conman. Does he just go round town trying to get free chickens, and that's what he does all day? And then what does he do with the chickens once he gets them? Or is this the first time it's actually worked? I suspect it is.

He coughs a bit while he thinks of something to say.

"Oh right, OK then. Yes. Thank you. I'll have it then."

"Righty-ho. I'll scan it as normal and that'll be that. However, I can't give you a receipt, as that would contravene the 'polluted goods surplus return as regards to poultry, and also you can't have a receipt' clause in our customer satisfaction policy."

He's starting to look anxious. "Yeah fine, whatever."

I pass the chicken over the scanner. Poor chicken. It could have gone to a respectable home and been Sunday lunch. I wonder if it was called Steve? I decide it was. Poor Steve. Oh wait, aren't chickens all women? Oh well, it doesn't matter now, Steve suits her.

I don't offer the man a carrier bag. He doesn't deserve 5p.

"OK then, here you go, and I'm sorry for any inconvenience caused. You have a lovely day now!"

Another face hurting grin.

The man walks away carrying Steve under his arm. I'm arguing with myself over this act of gross unprofessionalism.

Me: "That was grossly unprofessional."

Brain: "Buy a thesaurus. Anyway, he deserved it. He was a tit."

Me: "But I'll get in trouble for this if they find out!"

The chicken guy stands on a bag of crisps dropped by a kid, and continues without looking back or apologising. He leaves a trail of crisps on the floor.

When he gets to the door, the whole shop is filled with the kind of noise you'd describe as music if you were called 'Crusher McGee' and you had brain damage. He doesn't get far (chicken guy, not Crusher McGee). Whoops – I guess I forgot to take the security tag off the chicken, thus proving, for the first time ever, that chickens need security tags.

Chicken guy pauses for a split second, as you do when a shop alarm goes off, but then keeps walking, as casually as you can while carrying a dead chicken called Steve.

"Nick!" I yell. I'm good at yelling. "Nick! That man hasn't paid for that chicken!" It's technically correct.

Nick puts down *CROCHET GIRL!* and blocks chicken guy's path.

"I'm sorry sir, would you mind coming back into the store for a minute?"

Security guards shouldn't talk like that. They should talk like Steven Seagal. Nick should be busting the guy's ass right now and saying chicken puns at him:

"Cock-a-doodle… DEAD!"

"Why did the chicken cross the road? TO GET HIS ASS BUSTED!"

"Looks like you bought the farm… THE CHICKEN FARM!"

I'll have to make do with him politely apprehending the man and calling the police. He'll probably crochet him a nice pair of handcuffs to keep him apprehended and snug.

Chicken guy starts shouting, which of course doesn't help his case. Nothing says 'I'm mental' more than shouting 'I'm not mental!' He points at me:

"She gave me the chicken! That one there!"

Nick looks over at me.

"No he stole it!" I shout back. He said if I didn't let him take the chicken, he'd come back later and punch me in the leg!"

Nick takes my side, just as he should. He sits down with chicken guy, who is now threatening to sue me. Unfortunately for chicken guy, it's hard for legal threats to be taken seriously when they're punctuated with the phrase "this is fucking bollocks".

The police arrive and escort the man away; he'll probably get life in prison.

And Steve gets to be evidence. Well done Steve.

CROCHET GIRL! Jesus Christ.

2. PISS

I get home from work to find Joanne standing on her head calling me a fucker.

"Arse wanking son of a pube!"

I really wish she'd time her yoga for when I'm not around. The room is still coated in Dulux 'Fucking Yellow', but at least it doesn't stink of shit any more. I throw my coat onto the floor, where it lives. "Do you want a cup of tea?"

"YOU FUCKING BITCH TURD! Oh hiya, yes please."

Tea. Tea is the answer to everything. Tea is the answer to 'Why do I have such a shit job', and 'What is that brown stuff on the walls'. Let's make tea.

Wisely I picked up a bottle of vodka before I left work. I get free bottles from work, because I'm staff and I don't write them on the stocktaking list, so Karen assumes they were stolen, because she's nice and not a prick like me. Tea and vodka is an odd-tasting combination, but I've had worse.

"Stupid arsing fucking cuntparrot!"

Her swears are getting more creative. A couple of weeks ago she discovered this thing called 'Rage Yoga'. It's what it sounds like. You get in a yoga pose, fanny over head, then scream swears at the world. She claims it does her good.

Where's my Daniel O'Donnell mug? She better not have used it. I've spent eight hours trying not to tell people to fuck off, and I come back to this. It won't do.

I need Daniel O'Donnell. All the other mugs are in the sink and smell like dead bodies. I can't cope with it.

I storm back into the living room and fart, which is not what I'd planned to do.

"Have you had my Daniel O'Donnell mug?"

"No."

Oh God I did not just see her flaps. At least she's stopped shouting that she's going to kick my teeth in.

"Are you sure? It's not in the kitchen."

"Yes I'm sure! God, use another one!"

"There isn't another one. There are only dead bodies." I'm not going to let this go. "I haven't had it, so you must have had it."

Silence.

"You have had it haven't you?"

"Fucking fuck! Ommmmmm…"

She's still balancing on her shoulders with her arse in the air.

"Come on, think, I really need to find Daniel."

"I'm busy!"

I'm sick of this, so I kick her over. "There. You're not busy now. Help me find Daniel."

I march back into the kitchen and start opening the same cupboards I checked two minutes ago.

"Daniel!" I shout. "Daniel, where are you? I'm worried about you!" As I search I take swigs from my vodka bottle.

No Daniel. I look back into the living room to see Joanne doing what she calls the 'dead fish'. She's lying face down on the floor. That's not yoga, that's being lazy. "Joanne, stop sleeping! This is serious, I have a serious problem. Don't make me kick you over again because I'll try. And it won't be easy to kick you over while you're lying down so I'll have to kick you really fucking hard."

Her reply is muffled by the carpet. "If you come near me I'll kick you in the fanny."

I don't know what to do then, so I start crying a bit. Then I remember that man getting busted for stealing a chicken and I start laughing a bit. Then I remember that he didn't really steal the chicken, and also that Daniel O'Donnell is missing, and I start crying a bit again. Then I have some more swigs of vodka.

Joanne has stopped being a dead fish, and has seen my vodka.

"Oh, booze! Can I have some?"

She's being nice now that I have booze.

"Help me find Daniel and then you can have some of my booze."

She hesitates. "Actually I've gone off the idea. I don't want any."

She's being shifty. She's definitely being shifty. She knows where Daniel is and she's not telling me.

"You do fucking know where Daniel is! If you don't tell me what you've done with him, right now, I'm going to hit you with several pans."

The next few minutes are spent yelling incomprehensibly at each other, until I say "Right that's it, I'm going to look in your room. You've got him and I'm going to rescue him!"

"No! You're not allowed in my room! It's private!"

"WHAT HAVE YOU DONE WITH MY DANIEL O'DONNELL MUG!"

"I DID A PISS IN IT!"

What?

"What?"

"I did a piss in it. I was really mad at you the other day so I pissed in your Daniel O'Donnell mug. Happy now?"

I immediately assume the manner of a parent that's 'not angry, just disappointed'. "Is there piss in it now?"

"No, what do you think I am? I cleaned it but it still smells a bit of piss."

I let my brain process this information for a few seconds.

"You have... killed... my Daniel O'Donnell mug."

"A bit."

I plop down onto the settee.

"I'm sorry," says Joanne. "It was when you deleted all my *Ancient Aliens* off the Sky box. I'll go get it."

She slopes off upstairs. I'm too pissed to be properly upset, but I'm not so drunk that I'll use a mug that smells of wee. However, the thought of extracting another mug from the Jenga pile of chaos and misery that is our sink is too much for me.

Sighing, I head back to the kitchen to put the kettle on and find a pan.

3. FRENCH

I didn't quite make it to bed last night, but I did make it to the living room floor, which is where I stayed. Lifting my head is beyond me. I think my liver has collapsed. My eyes might be the wrong way round in my head. Daniel O'Donnell is lying on his side, staring at me.

"Stop judging me Daniel O'Donnell." I turn his face away from me. He smells of bleach now, which is better than smelling of wee.

Joanne is nowhere to be seen. She's probably still being shamefaced in her room. Good.

I don't have to be at work just yet. I'll have a bit more sleep.

When I wake up again, it's fucking red alert. I look at the clock, which is my first mistake. Then I figure out I'm massively late for work. That's my second mistake.

Also, I'm still a bit hammered. What do?

Before I do anything, I crawl to the kitchen and rest my head on the middle shelf of the fridge for ten minutes. It doesn't help much, but I do spot a cheese single stuck to the top shelf.

I think maybe I should have a small hair of the dog, just to get myself sorted out before work. Where's my vodka?

Shit, I drank all the vodka last night. The empty bottle is poking out from under the settee. Daniel O'Donnell is laughing at me. "Shut up Daniel." I kick him to the other side of the room. Then I remember I need him because all the other cups and glasses are in the sink and are covered in nuclear waste. Then I remember I can't drink out of him anyway because he's been soiled by bleach and wee. But I still want him around.

"Come back Daniel!" Shit, now I'm crying. Stop fucking crying. Pull yourself together.

Right. Shit. No booze. If I were me, where would I keep any spare booze?

There is no booze in the following places:

- The fridge
- The washing machine
- Under the sink
- In the drawer where we keep the carrier bags

"Daniel!" I shout. "Daniel, where is some booze please?"

Daniel must have heard me, because right at the back of a cupboard is half a bottle of ouzo. The lid looks like it was glued on several years ago, but I'm sure it's fine. Right, I'll just have a swig of this and I'll be right as rain.

An hour later and I might be a bit hammered again. I risk having another look at the clock. Shit, it's a hundred! Wait no, I mean one o'clock. Do I? Whatever, I'm late.

I'm going to have to bite the bullet and phone in to work. I should have been there a few hours ago. Luckily I have Karen's mobile number, so I don't have to bother ringing the shop. Should I text her? Don't want her to know I'm pissed. I try saying some sentences out loud. Daniel looks at me reproachfully.

"Alright Daniel, God, I'll text her. Happy?"

I try several times to write a text saying I can't come in because I'm ill, but each time my predictive text turns it into "Ayer Y can't cove unfinish shown today in I'm." An attempt to turn my predictive text off goes a bit wrong, and I end up setting the default language to French. I don't know French so I can't change it back. Fuck it, I'll worry about it later. I'm sure the French for 'Karen' is still 'Karen'.

It is, so I get her number up on the screen and press call.

"Hello, Karen Morrison."

"Yes hello?"

"Mel? Where are you?"

"What? Hello. This is Mel."

"Are you OK? Where are you, are you at home?"

That's a lot of questions in one go. I can answer the first one at least.

"It's Mel."

"Where are you? Bloody hell, you were supposed to be here ages ago. Where are you?"

"I'm OK. I'm ill. I can't come in."

"Oh God, I wish you'd have let me know earlier. What's the matter with you?"

I can't tell her I'm pissed. What do I say?

"I fell off."

"What?"

"I mean… I fell off. Hello? I'm not well. I fell off."

"What does that mean? What's up with you?"

"…Who is this?"

"Mel what the hell are you talking about? Why aren't you coming in? You're not making any sense."

"Oh it's Karen! I see. Yes. I fell off. But it's OK, I have a… (shit, I can't think of the phrase 'doctor's note') I have an invoice."

"What?"

I don't reply. I'm tired.

"Mel? Look, do you need me to call someone for you?

What's the matter with you?"

"My phone's gone all in French."

There's a pause.

"Are you… are you drunk?"

"No I told you, I'm fell off."

Another pause. "Mel, I think you've been drinking. In fact I'm sure you have and I don't want to know. I'm going to put you down as ill for today, but you'd better be in tomorrow, and we'll say no more about it. I'll cover for you this time, OK?"

This is the wrong time to start giggling down the phone.

"Mel! Are you listening?"

"What? Hi Karen. Yes tomorrow."

A sigh. "Right."

The phone goes dead. That was rude of Karen.

4. NURSE

When I wake up later on, my first thought is that whatever this is on my face fucking stinks. What is it?

It's the carpet. That'll teach me to vac without shaking. And also to spill that stuff on the carpet two weeks ago.

That's a good memory. I love that song. "Do the shake and vac and put the freshness back…"

Joanne is stood over me, holding a nurse outfit.

"Are you… singing? Seriously? Wake up!"

My first thought is that I'm dead and that a nurse has come to… no, wait, I can't be dead, I need a piss. Dead people don't need a piss, I don't think. I don't know, I've never been dead. If I ever am dead, I want it to be better than this stupid cow stood over me with a small nurse.

"I got you this."

I can't cope with this, my head is the wrong way round. She can fucking fuck off and I need a sherry and to not be alive.

"Where."

Then I feel Joanne's foot on my tit. This is both painful and erotic, and I don't want it to be.

"Where?"

"For fuck's sake, are you even alive?"

16

I don't know the answer to this question. I might very well not be. Who am I to answer that? I need to phone a call centre or something.

That gives me a brilliant idea, which I immediately forget.

Back to the situation at hand. Joanne's still holding a small nurse.

"Why do you have a small nurse."

"What?"

"A small nurse. Why do you have her. Or him. Or it. I'm not sure any more. What's the correct term for a tiny nurse in your hand and I have no idea what is fucking going on."

No reply.

"Daniel O'Donnell doesn't smell of piss any more."

"Yes, I bleached it again, It doesn't smell of piss any more I think. I wanted to apologise so I got you this."

Joanne says some other stuff, but I'm distracted by thinking about would a wasp vote UKIP.

I wake up a bit then. The wasp/UKIP thing isn't sorted out, so I make a note to come back to it later. I try to make sense of why Joanne is holding a nurse.

"You got me a nurse to apologise for pissing in my mug?"

"Yes. Well, it's just an outfit. There isn't actually a nurse in it. You have to be aware of that."

"You got me a nurse outfit."

"Yes I did."

"You could have got me another mug. Another Daniel O'Donnell mug."

"They don't do them in Home Bargains. I was there getting my lighters, and I saw this."

Why would they sell nurse outfits in Home Bargains? Maybe if I pay attention I'll be able to figure this out. Also if I sit up it might help.

Joanne goes to sit on the sofa with the nurse while I try to put my kidneys back where they're supposed to be. Now that I'm at eye level with the nurse outfit, I read the label.

"This is a child's nurse outfit."

"No, it's a sexy nurse outfit, suitable for hen nights and fun."

"It says 'age 8–11' on it."

"No it doesn't."

"It does. You see there, where it says 'age 8–11?' That's the bit where it says 'age 8–11' on it."

"God, it doubles up then! For God's sake!" She's rolling her eyes at me now.

I'm really confused. What's worse, that she bought me a child's nurse outfit, or that she thought she was buying me a sexy nurse outfit? Or that she pissed in my Daniel O'Donnell mug?

This is my fault. I shouldn't have deleted all that conspiracy shit off the Sky box. Then none of this would have happened. I'd still be hungover though, which is my main problem. I probably need a food as well.

"Have we got a food?"

Joanne thinks for a minute. "No, I don't think we have. There was some cheese in the fridge, but I ate that."

"Well, we need to get a food then."

"I'll get us a McDonald's?"

Joanne's offering to buy me a McDonald's. Why is Joanne offering to buy me a McDonald's?

"Why?"

"Why what?"

"Why are you suddenly buying me loads of stuff?"

She shrugs. "I still feel bad about Daniel. And it's not loads of stuff. Anyway I quite fancy some chicken nuggets. Come on, you're dressed enough. Put some trousers on though."

I let her drag me out of the door and up the road. Our McDonald's is only a couple of hundred yards away. You'd think we'd eat all our meals there, but I can never be arsed to go and Joanne is a vegan unless she's been on her bong. Tonight she's not being a vegan. She's singing a stupid made up song about chicken nuggets, although the more I hear it the more I realise she's nicked the tune to 'Lady In Red'.

She stops singing as we get to the car park. "By the way, I wanted to talk to you about something."

I fucking knew it. She wants a favour. That's why she's buying me food. It might be why she bought me the nurse outfit too, although she might have just been off her tits this afternoon.

5. NOT FISH

McDonald's is empty apart from a woman flirting with the guy behind the counter. Fuck's sake. Now he's going to resent us for interrupting his party, and he'll probably poison our food. Maybe he'll jizz in it. I'll get a Happy Meal. He wouldn't dare jizz in a Happy Meal.

We employ the British method of getting attention, which is to stand one to two feet away from the counter and look awkward until staff guy notices us. I look beyond the counter to see a woman hitting something with a tea towel. Staff guy is still flirting with the woman, who has now grabbed his collar.

Joanne starts laughing.

"What?"

"Sshhh. Listen."

I tune in on the conversation between staff guy and his girlfriend.

"I told you. NOT FISH!"

Staff guy mutters something and the woman giggles.

We do the decent thing and move closer to the pair, in order to accidentally overhear more.

"So... what *do* you want to order?"

"How many times do I have to tell you – NOT FISH!"

"OK, not fish. How about you tell me what you would like?"

"Not fish, I told you!"

I think the woman might be off her face. I'm also starting to suspect she's not his girlfriend.

"What about a cheeseburger?"

"Cheese! What do I look like, some kind of cheese person!?!"

The argument rages on. Fish, cheese, fish, cheese, fish, cheese, NO!

Then we discover she's ordering for her friend, who's asleep in a corner. Judging by the state of the friend, she wouldn't mind fish or cheese. I wouldn't put money on her not being dead.

I need a sit down. My hangover won't even begin to go away until I eat a big food, but this plan's being hindered by this mental fish cheese woman. I wonder if that corner is where you put your friends who need a lie down? It might be like a crèche. I wonder if the friend will be too pissed to fight back if I kick her out of the way.

Joanne starts singing her chicken nuggets song again except, for reasons known only to her, this time it's an octave lower. The guy behind the counter looks like he'd pay me a fiver to smash his face in and put him out of his misery. That's a shame, because I was thinking of offering him the same deal. The song prompts fish cheese woman to make her mind up.

"Yes, chicken nuggest! Five chicken nuggest!"

"Excellent choice madam" says Joanne.

Why can't she ever mind her own fucking business? She has to stick her nose in everywhere and piss in my stuff and get up in my business. I hate her. I want my Happy Meal.

Things like this never end well. Joanne intervenes in

mad people's lives and then I'm automatically involved just because I'm stood next to her and I live with her and I know her name. Ever since that woman in that pub accused us both of being CID then pulled our hair, I've learned to do the whole 'I'm not with her' routine. If fish cheese woman starts anything with Joanne I'm going to hide in the toilet.

"SHUT UP, THIS IS CURRENCY!"

Fish cheese woman is trying to pay for the "nuggest" with her friend's car keys. A routine inspection of the friend confirms that she's still asleep/dead on the seat.

She turns to Joanne for backup. "This is currency isn't it. Look at it. Are you telling me this isn't currency?"

"No I'm fucking not telling you that," says Joanne. She turns to the guy behind the counter. "This is currency, you should take it. Look how shiny it is." She takes the keys from fish cheese woman's hand and waves them in front of the guy. "Wooooooooooo!". She must have been doing her bong while I was asleep.

They both turn to me for my opinion. I now have a few options:

1. Agree with whatever they say and hope they both inexplicably die
2. Disagree and hope fish cheese woman doesn't know karate
3. Never eat anything ever again

Before I can settle on option 4 (get that silica gel out of my handbag and eat it), the door opens and a policeman comes in. Thank God, he's come to apprehend the woman and make her do 10–20 in the big house.

He does no such thing. He just orders a coffee, like nothing out of the ordinary is happening. The poor guy behind the counter has to ask him to do his bloody job before he serves him. His way of apprehending the felon is to laugh and say "Have we been to a party tonight?" Joanne, in a rare moment of sanity, has stopped encouraging the woman and has come to stand next to the colouring pages with me

The woman responds by trying to play a tune on the policeman's helmet with a pair of straws. Her legal defence? "Hahahahaha, I'm so pissed!!!!" The friend pipes up from her corner – "Me too! Hahahahaha". This makes us immediately shit bricks as we'd forgotten she was there.

When the policeman suggests the woman might like to go outside for "a nice chat", she starts accompanying her impromptu drum solo with choruses of "FUCK DA POLICE!" After this the 'nice chat' becomes more mandatory. He escorts fish cheese woman out to his car to the accompaniment of loud boos from her friend, who then goes back to sleep.

I'm going to have two Happy Meals now, safe in the knowledge that the guy will not have jizzed in them.

6. UNCLE JEFF

The next day I manage to successfully avoid Karen until she arrives at the shop, then I can't avoid her any more. She doesn't look pregnant yet; I mean, she hasn't got a baby hanging out of her or anything. This means she's probably going to be in a bad mood. If I'd been keeping up with my diet, I might have been able to hide behind the chewing gum rack. But I haven't, so I can't. Plus she's bound to come behind the counter sooner or later.

She smiles but doesn't say anything, and disappears into the staff room. I stuff the Rolo wrappers into my back pocket before I have to pay for them.

I'm not ready to get a lecture from her yet. She's going to say "You were out drinking with Joanne weren't you?" and I'll probably say "Yes, yes I was", even though that's not true. Then she's going to tut at me and give me that 'I'm not angry, I'm just disappointed' look, and spend the rest of the morning crapping on to me about fertility charts and niacin, as if I give a fuck about any of it.

Is there a way to sleep but still be stood up with your eyes open? I'll ask Joanne when I get home. I know before she got into the rage yoga thing that she was doing some mindfulness bollocks that involved chanting while doing colouring. She stopped that after she had a bad bong hit and became convinced the colours were going to get her.

"So what happened yesterday?"

Shit I didn't see Karen come back in. Truth? Lie? Pretend I didn't hear her? Can't do that, she's stood right in front of me. What did I tell her? I barely remember phoning in. This is one of the worst things about drinking booze; you have to backtrack and come up with something vague enough to cover your arse. Of course, that doesn't outweigh the best thing about drinking booze, which is that you get pissed.

"I'm sorry. I... had some bad news."

That might very well be true. I could have been told I had exploding fanny disease, and I wouldn't have remembered.

"Oh, I see..."

She waits for me to continue, when I thought that was a pretty good end to my excuse. What does she want, blood?

Right, quick-fire round time. What's some news that's bad enough to have made me start drinking ouzo yesterday, but not bad enough for me to still be off today? Is it:

A. 'I lost my job.' This is by far the stupidest thing my brain has ever done.

B. 'I've got six months to live.' If I did, the last thing I'd do is turn up to work at the fucking Co-op.

C. 'Joanne's got six months to live.' No, because that would be Joanne's bad news, not mine, and I'd have had to give her my ouzo. Also I wouldn't care.

D. The 'someone else is ill' thing is quite good though.

"My uncle Jeff. He's got six months to live."

"Oh God I'm sorry. Can I ask what's that matter with him?"

You can ask lady but I'm fucked if I know. Fuck, what's a really bad illness, quick! Bum cancer? Fuck off brain.

"Leprosy."

Oh well fucking done.

It turns out that this is the best thing I could have said, because Karen is clearly thinking no one would ever make that up. They'd say something clichéd, like, well, not leprosy anyway.

"Oh my God, the poor man. I'm sorry, I don't really know anything about… I didn't know people still got leprosy."

"Yeah, he'll pretty much just be a torso by Christmas."

Shit. I hope leprosy is the one where your arms and legs fall off. Too late now. I should have gone with bum cancer. I don't even have an uncle Jeff. Even if she doesn't believe me, Karen is far too polite to flat out call me a liar.

"Well if there's anything I can do you just let me know OK?"

"Oh yes but I'll be fine thank you. You do what you can. I'd rather not talk about it too much if you don't mind."

"Oh yes, of course." She huffs and smiles and that resets the conversation. "So, have we been busy?"

"No, not really."

"Oh, well that's good I suppose, what with your news and everything."

I rack my brain for something to say that will steer Karen away from 'my news'. Anything that isn't 'I'd like to stop talking now, please go away.' Pretty much the only thing that will get the conversation back to safety is Karen's never-ending quest to be pregnant.

"You know, I meant to tell you. I was reading the paper the other day, and there was a bit about supplements and conception…"

This does the trick. Karen immediately launches into three non-stop paragraphs about something she's started taking called 'Cassanovum Plus'.

"It's nettle leaf, which apparently tones and nourishes the uterus…"

I get a mental image of Karen's uterus lifting weights.

"And the royal jelly one can be inserted like a pessary…"

Is it time to go home yet.

7. IMPORTANT WORK

The living room stinks of incense. This is a bad sign. It means Joanne is working. Balls. I was going to sit in my own filth and watch *The Walking Dead* tonight. That plan's all gone to bollocks now.

Her laptop's there, along with her bells and her weird knife thing and Christ knows what else. She's taken over the entire sofa and floor but she's not in the room. A farting noise comes from upstairs, followed by laughter.

Daniel O'Donnell is still where I left him yesterday, but I think I'm going to have to retire him now. He still smells of bleach, and I don't know what's worse, drinking bleach or drinking piss. I'd probably be taking my life into my hands by drinking out of Daniel now.

Oh God I've just had an amazing idea. What if I do the washing up? Then I'd have some cups and stuff.

"What do you think Daniel? Should I do the washing up or what?"

Daniel gives me a twinkly smile. I take that as a yes.

"Come on then, you're helping." I pick Daniel up and take him with me into the kitchen.

"God Daniel, this was a stupid idea."

Why don't we have a normal kitchen? We don't have

one of those long jars for spaghetti. We don't have a, I dunno, a coffee masher. We've barely got a kettle since I bet Joanne a fiver she wouldn't boil beer in it and drink the beer. Fuck the washing up. If Daniel wants the washing up to get done that much, let him bloody do it.

Joanne starts talking at me while I'm still in the kitchen. "This poor guy's having awful trouble with his vibrational core. I need to unblock his crown chakra and that should stop his neighbours being so noisy."

I know she's just said words at me, but I'm fucked if I can get anything beyond that.

"Now I'm going to do a circle."

Again, what. It's been two years and I still don't know exactly what her job is supposed to be. I know it vaguely involves talking a load of crap about vibrations, ringing a bell and then charging people money.

"If you're staying in here I'll have to cleanse you with sage."

Oh God she's in it for the evening then. "You are not waving that sage shit near me again, it fucking stinks. Can't you do this in your room?"

"No, there's too much turbulence in there. I left my hairdryer plugged in last night so the ions are all over the place, but it should be back to normal frequency tomorrow."

Oh yeah, I forgot. This is why I drink.

"Anyway sorry, but I've already emailed this guy and told him I was going to do his vibrations tonight, so I have to now. I can't not do it, that would be really unprofessional, and sometimes it's dangerous."

This is bullshit. "Why haven't you done the washing up?"

"I had to clear a blockage in a woman's wood meridian."

"That's not a good reason!" I'm fucking sick of this. She

hasn't washed up and I can't drink out of Daniel O'Donnell because of her, so that means I'm down to minus one cups, I think. "You know what would have happened if you hadn't bothered doing whatever it is you did? Fucking nothing, that's what."

"That is so not true."

"It is fucking true, it's the truest thing I've ever said. You know what else is true? You should have done the fucking washing up. What are you going to do, think nice thoughts about the washing up until it's somehow magically clean?"

"Why are you so stressy tonight? You need to do some anal breathing."

"Anal? What?"

"Anal breathing. It would do you the world of good. It draws energy up from the Earth's core and up through your chakras, and expels negativity."

"Expels? Are you telling me to go have a poo?"

She rolls her eyes. "The anus is incredibly powerful. It isn't just to do with that stuff you know."

"Whatever. I'm not doing anything with my arse. Now are you going to do the washing up or not?"

"I can't right now! God, I'll get to it but I have work to do!"

Before I can reply she picks her bell up and starts ringing it. I fucking hate her. Right that's it. I'm off to the shop, and I'm going to buy a load of wine and Doritos, and she can't have any. I'm going to get pissed in my room and read my *Beano* annuals.

8. FAX

Joanne knocks on my door later that evening. "Guess what?"

"No. Piss off."

Silence. I think she's gone.

"Guess what?"

Oh.

"Fucking what!"

"I washed up."

"Right, OK."

"Don't be like that. I made you some supper if you want it."

This is new. I stick one eyeball round the door. She's holding some kind of sandwich.

"I didn't know we had bread?"

"Yeah, we've probably got about twelve slices, if you count these."

"Where did it come from?"

"I bought it, obviously."

I open the door and take the plate from her hands. "Well... thanks. Yeah. Ta. What is it?"

"It's a sandwich."

"Yeah I know that. What's in it?" I examine it but I

31

can't see any filling.

"Butter."

"Yeah what else?"

"What?"

"What else?"

"Oh. Did you want something else in it then?"

I didn't want anything in it to start with. I never asked for a sandwich. "So it's just bread and butter really then isn't it."

"Yeah but I made it into a sandwich."

She looks quite proud of this. Fuck it, at least she made an effort. And at least she washed up.

"Let's eat it in your room. I want to ask you about something."

She has made me a 'sandwich'. I suppose I should listen.

I sit back down on my bed and eat my bread while Joanne starts rooting through my bras. She holds up a leopard print one that I might as well use as a hair bobble now for all the good it would do.

"My tits would look amazing in this."

"Have it. It hasn't fit me for ages."

"Really? Ace." She puts the bra on over her t shirt then sits on the bed.

"So what's this thing you wanted to ask me?"

"I've booked us a holiday!"

"That's not a question. And what do you mean a holiday?"

"A camping holiday! It's all paid for, sort of. You just have to pay for your half."

I've never been camping in my life. I'm not sure why she thinks I'd want to go camping. I especially don't know why she thinks I'd want to go camping with her. I can barely manage living in a house with her a lot of the time. Before I can stop it I get a mental image of having to sleep with my face next to Joanne's fanny. Nope.

"I don't really fancy camping, sorry."

"But camping's brilliant! Is it tents you're scared of?"

Why does she think I'm scared? Who does that?

"Why would I be scared of tents? I just don't want to go camping."

"Have you ever been camping?"

"No, because I don't like camping."

Joanne helps herself to a swig of my wine. "That's stupid. How do you know you don't like camping if you've never been camping?"

"It's just never appealed to me."

"Haven't you ever been to a music festival or anything?"

"No. I don't see the point of them. I've seen them on TV. It's just mud and songs that don't sound as good as they do on the CD."

"God no, it's more than that. It's open spaces and drinking beer and meeting new people. It's no rules for the whole weekend. It's getting back to nature."

"Great. No rules and shitting in a hole."

She tuts. "You do not shit in holes. They have toilets."

"Well it's hardly getting back to nature then. Nature doesn't include Portaloos and expensive beer. Anyway, are you even talking about a festival?"

"Yeah. It's not really a rock festival though. It's more of a… folk festival. It's more acoustic. In fact, they like you to bring your own instruments and join in."

"Still no. Sorry, I really don't want to spend a weekend banging a tambourine."

She's quiet for a minute. She's plotting her next move. Why is she so bothered about taking me? She's got other friends. They're weird, frightening people that I don't really like having in the house, but still. I want this conversation to end so I can get back to my wine. Also, I was in the middle of a really good *Minnie The Minx* story. She was just about to break some plates.

"Why don't you go with Bonnie? Or that guy Spaz?"

She sighs. Bonnie's still got her tag on. And it's not *Spaz*, as you know perfectly well. It's *Spoz*. And I can't go with him."

"Why? I think you'd be safe with him. I doubt he'd know what to do if it got to that stage."

"No, it's not that…"

There are bits of this I don't know yet. She didn't just decide to suddenly go camping. I wish she'd get on with it so I can say no and she'll go away. I only have about another hour of drinking before I have to go to bed.

She sighs. Awkward head scratching. "The thing is…"

If I kick her she might speed the fuck up.

"…I've met someone. Sort of."

My first thought is 'what's this got to do with camping'. My second thought is 'fucking hell'.

"What, a man?"

Against my better judgement, I'm suddenly interested. As far as I know, Joanne hasn't had a boyfriend since I've known her. I'm sure that guy Spoz fancies her, but apart from that I'm drawing a blank.

"Yes, a man, with a head and arms and a penis and everything. He has such wonderful vibrations." She's grinning now. I can practically smell her planning some horrible hippy wedding. "He wants me to go to this festival with him." She pauses. "That's the thing though, I don't know him that well yet. I don't want to go on my own so he can murder me."

"What, and you think I'm going to be any help if you get murdered?"

"Well he'll probably think twice about murdering two of us. Look he's not gonna be a murderer anyway."

Christ. She wants me to go and be a third fucking wheel on a date in a tent. With someone who's 'probably' not a murderer.

"What's his name?"

"Well, his birth name is Steven, but he prefers to be called Fax."

"Fax? As in fax machine?"

"No no. You see, Fax is a Latin word meaning 'fire' or 'flame of love'. He says it's an energizing name, and he's seen loads of positive changes since adopting 'Fax', and that his aura feels a lot more tuned in to the elements. He feels vigorous."

What. Where is my wine.

"Where did you meet him?"

She starts grinning again. "We've been chatting for ages. We met on Above Top Secret. I was trying to find out about the humming in Bristol, and so was he. Then I found out he goes on my lightworker forum, and in fact we must have been chatting to each other without knowing!"

She looks at me, as if expecting me to know what 1% of those words meant. What's a secret? Bristol?

"You two met online?" I think I've managed to get that right at least.

"Yeah," she sighs. "And that's the thing really. I mean, I'm almost certain I love him, but there's still that thing about what if he isn't who he says he is? What if he's some weirdo? Or an old woman? Or a people smuggler?"

Wait, she *loves* him? I'm still... the bastard, she's finished my wine!

"My wine!"

"What? Oh sorry." She tries to look concerned. "I'll buy you some more."

Like hell she will. She'll buy me another child's outfit or some other fucking nonsense. She once bought me a pencil to say sorry for using my mobile to call somewhere in America.

"Anyway I really think this Fax thing is more important right now. I won't know if I love him or not until I've met him."

It clicks then. "Wait, you haven't even met him yet?"

She tuts. "That's what I've been trying to tell you!"

"Wait, what was that about Bristol then?"

"What? Oh that doesn't matter. The point is, you have to come with me so please come with me. Then I can decide whether to love him or not."

This is not how relationships are supposed to work. Aren't you supposed to go out with someone for ages before you love them? And since when do you 'decide' to love someone?

I'm tired of this anyway. "Look he won't be a murderer. Just go on your own."

"I caaaaan't!" God I hate it when she starts whining."

"Yes you can. Look, I don't like camping and you've finished my wine. I'd like to go to bed now, so off you piss. Go on."

"Look please! I can't go on my own! He's not going on his own, he's going with a bunch of people, so I have to go with a bunch of people. I can't just turn up on my own and expect to hang out with them! I have to be cool about this!"

Be cool? When did she start being the Fonz? And I'm not 'a bunch of people'.

"Please, I need you to come with me. Together we'd be a group!"

"No, together we'd be a duo. A really shit duo."

I can't see this finishing any time soon, short of physically carrying Joanne out of my room and depositing her downstairs. I say the only thing I can think of to get her to leave it for tonight:

"Let me think about it OK? Let me go to bed and think about it."

I mean this in the same way parents mean 'We'll see', but she's taken this as a yes, judging by her face which is now gurning with happiness. She finally fucks off. It's probably better that she finished my wine; trying to deal with customers when you have a hangover is a bitch.

9. LOVE LETTER

So far, the most interesting thing that's happened today is watching two teenagers arguing over which of them had to try to buy a bottle of Lambrini. I could have saved them the bother and told them neither of them had any chance of getting served, but I quite like watching arguments. In the end they both chickened out and bought two cans of red bull. What a fucking pair of delinquents.

Six o'clock. I'm so bored. I wish some armed robbers would come in. My eyeballs keep swivelling towards the vodka bottles behind me. Would anyone be able to tell if I had a swig out of one? I could still sell it – if the customer complained I could just accuse them of already being pissed. Nick would back me up, and maybe kick the customer in the head. No he wouldn't. He'd just start reading *CROCHET GIRL!* again.

Probably not a good idea anyway; it's Slimming World later, I'll just have another packet of chewing gum. It's awful when you wish you could get pissed but you can't. Well fuck it. After my weigh in I'll get hammered. I'm off tomorrow, I can get hammered if I want to. I'll have something exotic, like a bottle of blue curaçao. That'll show them.

I need to figure out what I'm going to say to Joanne. If I flat out refuse to go camping, she'll just bother me the entire time. I should tell her yes then back out at the last minute, but my stupid conscience won't let me. Jesus, but I can't actually go. Folk festival. I don't even like folk music. Isn't it all done by fishermen wearing jumpers? While in theory it would be nice to get away for a bit, I can't think of anything worse than sitting round in a tent with Joanne and her weirdo boyfriend, banging a tambourine while they have sex.

I can't even begin to imagine what this guy Fax is like. I imagine that on his home planet people do things like call themselves 'Fax', and no one bats an eyelid. If they have eyelids. They might just be intelligent gas or something, I don't know.

I close my eyes and lean against the cigarette display. If I could be anywhere in the world right now, where would I be? The countryside does sound pretty nice, but the proper countryside, i.e. not a tambourine or a pair of bongos in sight. To me, the proper countryside is dark and brooding, like Heathcliff, except not when Cliff Richard played Heathcliff. That was just weird.

I wish we had a garden. I'd sit in it.

I can feel myself drifting off into thoughts of my fictional garden. Sitting in a deckchair at sunset, glass of wine in hand, listening to whatever birds hang round people's gardens. Chickens or something. And I don't have any neighbours, and that man doesn't walk up and down our street with his Lidl carrier bag. I try to add the whoosh of the sea in the distance, but it just ends up making me need a piss.

Suddenly the chicken starts laughing in a man's voice. I open my eyes to see Nick doubled over at something Joanne said. Oh Fucking Christing hell. Why is she here.

She has to come and bother me at work? I don't bother her at work, except that I live at her work, so I suppose I do. Still, my point stands. She can fuck off.

"No ha ha, I mean I'll realign your earth energies for you but don't ask me to do more than that, I'm spoken for now ha ha!"

Some more bollocks which I tune out. I try to think about my garden again, but now it's full of earth energies and dogshit.

"Yo, can I have this Creme Egg?"

What the fuck is she wearing. I think she's gone for 'Beyonce meets Caroline Lucas' today. She's eaten half the Creme Egg in one go, which is something only a psychopath would do.

My remaining thimbleful of optimism tells me she might, just might, only be here to buy a Creme Egg, and then she'll leave. "You never know," says the thimble. "She might not bring up the camping. She might have forgotten all about it."

"So you're coming camping right?"

I empty the thimble down the sink. "I don't know. Anyway, 50p."

"What?"

"50p."

"What's 50p?"

"The Creme Egg."

"What? You said I could have it!"

"I said no fucking such thing."

"You did, I said 'can I have this' and you agreed!"

"That's what people say when they want to buy something!" You're… look, just pay."

"Well I haven't got any coins or anything."

"Why not?"

"They make me allergic a lot of the time."

Like when you have to fucking pay for something.

"For Christ's sake, just pay for your sodding Creme Egg."

"I can't!"

I'm going to hit her with the Co-op. I'm going to pick up the entire Co-op and smack her in the face with it.

"Fine, I'll call Nick."

"Fine, Nick will just come and have sex with me anyway."

"I don't think he will."

"God, I don't see why you're so obsessed with getting coins anyway!"

"You do understand that the money isn't actually for me? I don't personally want it. The Co-op wants it. Otherwise you've stolen that Creme Egg."

"Well you don't have to tell anyone…"

I look at her.

"Well you don't!"

I look at her, but I put more effort into it.

"Fine! God!" She pulls a crumpled £50 note from her pocket.

"Fine, there. I want my change all in silvers please."

"You want £49.50 in silvers?"

"Yes please."

"Well tough shit. And what happened to you being allergic to coins all of three seconds ago?"

"Silver's OK. It's a moon metal."

"It's not real fucking silver! I – look. I'm not arguing with you any more." I shove a pile of notes and change towards her. "Take your money."

"Oh, I wanted to show you something as well."

What? What does she want to show me? Her fanny? Some soil she found that she's going to try and smoke?

"Fax sent me this."

She takes her iPad from her bag and shoves it in my face. Once I've pushed it back to more than two inches away from my eyeballs, I can see a photo of a man. Although 'photo' might be underselling it a bit. It's more like an extravaganza.

It looks like it was taken during one of those 'makeover and photo session' packages you sometimes win in raffles. He's standing shirtless in front of a purple cloth, looking at what I assume is something a bit interesting, like Ross Kemp trying on jackets. There's a zigzag across his face, which on closer inspection turns out to be his beard. It looks like he's done that on purpose.

What really gets my attention is the tattoos. One one arm he has two wolves howling at the moon. On the other arm is Jason Donovan. I swear it's Jason Donovan.

"Who's that on his tattoo?"

"Oh, that's some wolves."

"Yeah I know that. I mean on his other arm."

"Oh right yeah. Erm, it's either Jason Donovan or his brother, I forget which."

So there's a chance it actually could be Jason Donovan? Who does that?

"Yeah, something to do with his spirit animal."

"Jason Donovan is his spirit animal?"

"Or that might be the wolf one."

He looks a bit like Laurence Llewelyn-Bowen, if he'd gone insane one day.

"He sent me an email this morning." Joanne's now completely forgotten that she was livid with me two minutes ago for not giving her £49.50 in silvers.

With zero encouragement from me, she pulls up the email and starts reading aloud from it. She's either trying to put on a romantic accent and failing, or Fax is from West Bromwich.

"*Hello m'lady. I love that you're an early riser like me. I was doing my Tai Chi this morning and thinking about you. Then a squirrel bit me on the foot. You know how I feel about animal bites – all they do is allow the energy from the creature to flow into you. So I didn't interfere but now I'm limping a bit. Do you have time for some remote reiki later? Big pharma painkillers do nothing but mess with your head. I can't wait to be with you...*"

"Hang on Jo, move out of the way a bit." Agog at this as I am, two old dears are approaching the counter with a basket.

She steps to the side but carries on reading, completely oblivious to the fact that I am now serving Derek and Mavis.

"*...we can explore each other's carnal beings...*"

'Beep'. Tinned ham.

"*...You know, I've been chanting to Xochiquetzal, the sexuality Goddess...*"

'Beep'. Bran Flakes.

"*...Under this rowan tree I know. Rowan is a natural aphrodisiac...*"

'Beep'. Lurpak.

"*...The womb is so powerful. I love to draw from that energy...*"

'Beep'. Three pack of Polos.

At this point I can't tell if Derek and Mavis are deaf or just really polite.

"*...organic lube...*"

"FOR GOD'S SAKE SHUT UP!"

I'm glaring at Joanne. Derek and Mavis are glaring at me.

"Joanne I've got work to do. Will you please go home or something."

She huffs and puts her iPad back in her bag. Derek and

Mavis leave, powered by tutting and steam. I slump back against the cigarettes. I'm going to move away where she can't find me. I'll move to up a mountain. I'll live off the land and open a jam shop. Up a mountain.

"Here. Get a bottle or something, and maybe save me a bit if you have any later or something."

I open my eyes to see Joanne pushing a twenty to me across the counter.

"Sorry I bothered you at work. I was just really excited about Fax."

She leaves before I can think of a suitable response. God damn it, it's even worse when she's trying to be nice.

10. LARD

This is my ninth Slimming World meeting. I hope I've lost some weight. I only started coming here because I heard they gave out stickers, but I've never fucking seen any. They shouldn't only give you stickers for losing weight, it's not fair. They should give you at least five stickers for turning up and sitting through the dreary meetings. If we had our meetings in McDonald's or in the pub, a lot more people would stay till the end. Or, if you're slimmer of the week, you get to cook and eat the person you like least in the group, instead of getting a carrier bag full of second hand fruit.

I might be slimmer of the week this week, you never know. I mean, it has to happen sooner or later. It can't keep going to Mandy just because she manages to lose three stone every week. Just because she started out at 32 stone. That's just cheating.

"Oh dear, another gain." Marianne gives me this information with a smile, like she's pleased her crappy methods don't work. "I tell you what, stay after Image Therapy and we'll have a chat and I'll look at your food diary OK?"

This isn't a suggestion, this is an order. I haven't got a food diary. I've never got a fucking food diary, and even if

I filled one in it would be full of lies. Oh God, I don't want to 'stay after Image Therapy'. I don't want to 'have a chat'. I want to go home and drink my vodka. I push the bottle deeper into my bag and try to cover it up with used tissues and assorted crap. I wouldn't put it past Marianne to go through my bag in case I keep a block of lard in there for emergencies. Lard is frowned upon here, because it isn't carrot sticks. You're only allowed to eat carrot sticks on this diet; wanting to consume anything except 'yummy carrot sticks' is seen as weakness, and the guilty party is tutted at then shot out of a cannon.

Marianne gives me a pat on the arm then glides away to patronise some more fat women. I knob around by the tea and coffee, reading the poster about an upcoming trip to Drayton Manor. I know for a fact that at least seven of the women in this room are going to get stuck on all the rides, and will have to be removed using a crane.

'Clap clap clap' – "Shall we get started ladies?"

She always refers to us as 'ladies', choosing to ignore the five members of the group with penises. They don't seem to care. They just sit next to their wives with a faraway look in their eyes, as if to say 'In the olden days I would have been able to lock you in the coal hole for making me do this'.

We all sit round in a circle, praying the kids' plastic chairs will hold our weight.

"Laura has lost three pounds this week!"

Applause. Fuck Laura. I hate Laura.

"Judith has lost half a pound this week!"

Applause. Also fuck Judith. Half a pound isn't even a real thing.

"Oh dear, I'm afraid Melissa's gained a pound this week. Never mind, let's give her a clap for showing up and staying to class!"

Applause. I wish I was dead.

"So Melissa, what went wrong this week?"

My fucking life. That's what went wrong.

I shrug and look at the floor. "Um, dunno." I feel like I'm about to be sent to my room to 'think about what I've done'.

She smiles again. She's probably enjoying my hideous fat. She probably stands in front of the mirror at home and rubs herself all over with Flora Pro-Activ, muttering 'yummy, healthy carrot sticks' to herself.

I should have just gone straight home and started drinking. But I can't, because I paid for twenty non-re-fundable meetings up front. I'd quite like to go back in time and kill my past self for being such an idiot.

"Do you want to tell us about the McDonald's?"

What? What the fuck? How does she know I went to McDonald's?

She notes my look of confusion and terror.

"On Tuesday night you wrote on your Facebook profile that you'd just been to McDonald's."

Jesus Christ she's spying on me. I never gave her my Facebook. Does she also sneak into my house and test any spare wee lying around?

"I… how did you find my Facebook?"

"Do you remember when you filled in our joining form, and we asked for your email address?"

She stops there as if that's somehow an explanation.

"So… you searched for me on there?"

"That's right! Slimming World is passionate about its members' success, and we find that touching base with you online is an excellent way to spot problems as they appear."

"That's… I guess so."

Shit, she probably read my post about what I'd do to Andrew Lincoln with a Kit Kat. How many calories do you burn beating someone to death in an embarrassed rage? Right that's it. I'm never doing anything ever again in case she's watching me.

We move on before I can paranoid myself to death. This week's discussion is about diet substitutes. I pay a bit of attention, thinking it might be about where you can buy two calorie bread or something. No such luck. She's probably just going to do her usual party trick of telling everyone to eat carrot sticks.

"OK, can anyone tell me what this is?" Marianne is holding up a picture of a burger.

Someone puts their hand up. "It's a picture of a burger."

"Ha ha, yes that's right, but it's also the *concept* of a burger. Now, can anyone tell me if this burger is a good thing to eat?"

Someone else puts their hand up. "Probably not."

"Exactly! This burger should not be a part of your daily eating plan. However, there are a few things you can do to make this burger a lot more figure-friendly! Can anyone think of any?"

How about you fucking think of them for us, like you're paid to do. Fuck you, with your thin tits. And anyway, so far all this has done is make me really want a burger.

No one 'gets the ball rolling', so Marianne starts to reel off her list of instructions on how to ruin a burger.

"Now then, if we use two small slices of wholemeal bread instead of this yucky greasy bun, we can count the bread as our fibre for the day. But we don't want to be eating all that horrible fatty meat, do we?"

Everyone is now drooling on the floor, indicating that yes, they would like to eat that horrible fatty meat. After they've finished doing sex with it.

"So what I would suggest is making your own Slimming World burger patties using broccoli! Broccoli, or a similar green vegetable, is so easy to make into a patty."

When is a burger not a burger? When it's a fucking pile of broccoli and misery.

"Simply add your favourite herbs and spices – and remember, all herbs and spices are completely free on Slimming World!"

She pauses here as if expecting a round of applause for this. She doesn't get one.

She holds up the next picture. "Now, with summer approaching, it's time to talk about yummy, healthy holiday treats!"

Now we're being forced to look at a picture of a doughnut, fish and chips, and some ice cream.

"You can still enjoy treats like fish and chips – simply remove the batter from your fish, and swap the greasy chips for something healthy like baked beans!"

I'm now crying internally.

"As for the doughnut, try swapping it for a juicy, fresh apple. Full of the taste of summer!"

She doesn't seem to realise that we're all here because we view having to eat apples as a punishment.

"And, ladies, you can still indulge in a cheeky ice cream! Just swap the fattening vanilla whippy for a pot of frozen Muller Light!"

Because that's available from all good ice cream vans.

I can't take any more of this. I want to go home and get pissed on yummy, healthy vodka. But first we have to look at the 'snacks' picture: bag of crisps, bar of chocolate, bowl of peanuts.

"Now sometimes we aren't really hungry, we just want the feeling of munching on something. So when you really must munch, try munching on a big bowl of…"

She's going to say it. She is, she's going to say it.

"…carrot sticks!"

I'm surprised a fanfare didn't sound.

"Whilst carrot sticks are my personal favourite because they're so yummy, there's such a wide variety of healthful snacks you can choose. If carrot sticks aren't your thing – although why wouldn't they be ha ha – you could always try a handful of grapes, or some bean sprouts!"

I've never heard someone be so enthusiastic about bean sprouts.

Then she decides to have mercy on us and shoos us all out of the room. I make sure to shuffle along in the middle of the group so she doesn't spot me leaving. I'm not sure I could take sitting there listening to her tell me to eat carrot sticks instead of food. Anyway, vodka is made from potatoes, so I'm sure that counts.

11. HE-MAN

Joanne's reaction to Marianne's words of wisdom is "Ignore the fat cow." I might listen to her advice.

"Everyone knows that dieting is really bad, spiritually," says Joanne, opening a can of Carlsberg. "Your soul knows what weight your body is supposed to be at and if you try to go any lower it fights you."

"That's easy for you to say, you've always been four stone."

"I just try to eat things with positive vibrations."

"Like lager?"

"You don't *eat* lager. Anyway, look what I got off eBay." She passes a carrier bag to me. It's full of action figures.

"Fuck, this is brilliant! How much were these?"

"I dunno."

I empty the bag out on the floor so I can root through the contents. Wow. He-Man, Skeletor, some others who I'm sure are from the same show. A couple of Gladiators. If my memory is correct, these are called Jet and Snake. No, Cobra! God I used to be in love with Cobra. I examine his plastic crotch to see if the flames of desire are still burning. I don't think they are.

Another one who I don't know who he is but he has

interesting tits.

While I'm sorting through the figures, Joanne is pouring some of my vodka into her lager. That's disgusting, and it's a sign we'll end up doing something stupid. Fuck it, I'm off tomorrow. I'm going to have some vodka, but instead of lager I'm going to mix it with more vodka.

Since Joanne really did do the washing up, we now have three mugs. This makes me feel like the king of mugs. I revel in my new-found royal status and collect all three mugs from the kitchen, slopping vodka into each one. It doesn't matter which one I drink out of, they're all boring.

That reminds me. "Where's Daniel?"

"Who?"

"Daniel O'Donnell, where is he?"

"What? Oh your cup? I put it back in the cupboard."

"What? Don't put him in there! He's special, he doesn't belong with the minions."

I've failed to tell Joanne about my new status as king of the mugs. I've also failed to tell her that Daniel has been promoted to Lord Chamberlain. Also, she pissed in him, why would she put him back in the cupboard?

I rescue Daniel from the cupboard and put him on the floor next to me. I consider making some sort of crown for him, but dismiss this as stupid and crap.

Joanne joins me on the floor. "Do you want to play He-Man?"

I think about this for a minute. I realise that I'd like to play He-Man very much. I don't know if this should worry me since adults aren't supposed to want to play He-Man. They're supposed to want to do things like buy wallpaper.

"Can I be He-Man?"

"Fuck off, I'm being He-Man."

"What? That's not fair, you asked me to play so I should

get to be He-Man."

"No way. It's my He-Man so I'm being him. You can be Skeletor."

"I don't want to be Skeletor."

"Why not? Skeletor's cool."

"If he's so cool you be him and I'll be He-Man."

"No fuck off. I'm being He-Man and that's that. If you don't want to be Skeletor do you want to have an army of Gladiators?"

"Cobra and Jet isn't an army, and anyway Jet's rubbish. Jet can be on your side."

"You're just jealous of Jet."

"I just don't want to be Skeletor! Skeletor always loses!"

"He might not."

"He fucking will! They'll get in a battle and you'll say 'He-Man has to win because He-Man always wins because that's just how it is'.

"I will not! He-Man might have a cold or something."

I refill my mugs. Maybe I should let Joanne be king of He-Man if I'm going to be king of the mugs. I guess I might be able to compromise.

"Right, I'll be Skeletor. But Skeletor's going to be able to shoot fire out of his eyes."

"He can't do that –"

" – Out of his eyes *and* out of his arse."

My superior arguing skills have her over a barrel and she knows it. If she wants to play He-Man, she has to let Skeletor shoot fire out of his arse. Fair's fair.

"Fine." She finishes off her can. "We need to make Castle Grayskull too."

An hour later we've got a fantastic set-up going on. Joanne's handbag is now Snake Mountain, where we put people if they've been naughty. So far I've had to put Jet in there because she tried to Hang Tough Man-At-Arms to death. We've also got a pan of water, which is the 'magic lake'. We haven't figured out what the magic lake is for yet, apart from swimming in, but it's fun to make our guys do super high dives into it.

Castle Grayskull is a thing of beauty. We got my quilt from upstairs and decorated it with cans and loo roll.

Even though Joanne made me be Skeletor, I'm definitely winning thanks to Skeletor's 'shits of fire', which make He-Man go blind and insane. Joanne keeps complaining about this, but only because I'm winning. She makes He-Man run over to the magic lake and throws him in. When she takes him out again she declares that he now has 'magic water shield power', so the shits of fire are useless against him. Balls. That seems to be within the rules.

I decide to be proactive, so I turn my arm into Skeletor's mega-catapult. In other words, I'm going to throw stuff at He-Man. I start with an empty can. This makes little impact, so I throw a full can.

"Ow that fucking hurt!"

I can't reply, I'm laughing too much.

We declare a temporary ceasefire so we can get some more drinking done. Joanne lights the remains of a joint she finds under the settee. In between knocking back mouthfuls of vodka and trying not to immediately sick it back up again, I realise I'm having a good time, which is a feeling I'm not used to lately. We should do this more often. I'd forgotten that Joanne can be fun when she's not pissing in my stuff.

When I come back from having a wee, Skeletor is missing. So is Joanne, but that doesn't seem as important.

"Daniel, have you seen Skeletor?"

No reply.

I can't see Joanne or Skeletor in the kitchen. They're either upstairs or Joanne suddenly decided to go out. I hope they're not upstairs. Upstairs is where people go if they want to have sex. Is she going to have sex with Skeletor? Oh God I'm so hammered. I'll definitely have a glass of water after the battle is finished. But first I need to finish the battle. Shit, I thought we had more stairs than that.

Joanne's in her bedroom, next to the window. Skeletor's in her hand.

"You can't have Skeletor, the battle isn't finished! What are you doing with him anyway?"

"I'm throwing him into the bottomless pit!"

"You're going to throw him out of the window?"

"No, I'm throwing him into the bottomless pit!"

"Don't actually do that, because then he'll just be on the pavement, and you'll have to go get him."

"No, he'll be in the bottomless pit!"

I don't believe for one second that she'd really chuck Skeletor out of the window. She just wants to make me let her win the battle. I decide to perform what is a genius tactical move considering I've had a lot to drink.

"Fine, throw him in the pit, see if I care."

This is only one step away from 'I'm getting you done', but it might work and I might not lose the battle. It's not fair if she wins by cheating, and I'm pretty sure this counts as cheating somewhere. Anyway I don't see why He-Man automatically has to win just because he wears a bra.

She opens the window, and the next thing I know the cackling moron has thrown her own Skeletor figure out of the window. Shit. I guess she really wants to win the battle.

I hurry my fat drunk arse over to the window. "Where did he land? Can you see him?"

"No. You know what, I don't think he's really in the bottomless pit."

"I told you. You'd better go get him. Oh shit look!"

It's the man with the Lidl bag. He walks up and down

the street most evenings. He stops outside our house and picks something off the floor. It goes into the Lidl bag and he walks away.

I think something bad has just happened. Also, this raises new questions. Does that man just go round picking things up off the floor or what? Anyway, the main thing is that we're both hoping he's just picked up a random load of dogshit instead of Skeletor.

Joanne shoves me down half the stairs in her rush to get outside. It's funny how throwing someone into a pretend bottomless pit can sober you up.

There's no sign of the man. There's no sign of Skeletor. Joanne is crying.

"jvndiclkuiljekhhh!"

"Yes, I know."

"Incegkw cvghrhrenjchvstft!"

"Yes, I'm sure it is."

I don't know what else to do, so I pat her on the head and say 'there there'. Then I pour her some vodka to help replenish her fluids. I know you have to keep people's fluids up.

The vodka doesn't help, she's still inconsolable. I think I'm doing quite well not pointing out that she's a stupid idiot cow and I told her so. I don't think it's the right time. Maybe I'll write that bit into a speech to use at a surprise party I'll probably never bother throwing for her.

"If it helps, you definitely won. Skeletor was definitely vanquished and all that."

It doesn't help. Joanne retreats into her 'dead fish' pose on the floor.

"Hgfegfbhebfrkivhkehuh!"

Now's probably not a good time to kick her up the arse. I want to cheer her up. We were having fun before weird Lidl man came along and spoiled everything. And now

I'm not sure how she's even breathing, what with having a face full of carpet *and* all the crying.

I need to distract her. I need a plan. It's time to consult Daniel, because I'm far too pissed to think of anything good. Unfortunately, trying to make Daniel accompany me to the kitchen using my mind alone doesn't work, so I have to pick him up. Daniel's so lazy sometimes.

"Daniel, what do?"

He doesn't reply. Maybe he's mad at me. Maybe he's mad because I'm using another mug.

"Come on Daniel, this is too important for all that now. Think, damn you! Remember when she got upset and spent an hour trying to kick herself in the fanny? We do not want a repeat of that."

Daniel has a think while I finish off my vodka. Then I start to have an idea. I'm not sure it's a good idea. I run it past Daniel.

"So that's the plan. What do you think? Will it work?"

He gives me the twinkliest, most Irish grin yet.

"Oh good!"

I skip back into the living room. "Hey guess what?" I say to her upturned bum. "I've decided to come camping with you after all!"

This is OK because there's no way she'll remember this tomorrow.

She starts using real words again, which means I must have said the right thing. "Oh good. But I thought you didn't like camping?"

I think this is what she said, it's hard to tell since she's still face down on the carpet.

"Well I was thinking, and I could probably do with some fresh air and stuff. Come on, let's have a drink. Fax wouldn't want you to be upset."

She perks up when I mention Fax. "You'll really like

Fax. He's so wise. And he's a black belt. Apparently Steven Seagal refused to fight him in a dry cleaners once."

What.

She launches into a five minute monologue about Fax. Something about how he stopped the government banning carbon dioxide. I'm not sure the government would do that. And if they were going to do that, I'm not sure they'd change their plans because a man named Fax threatens to karate them.

12. MILLETS

I slept in Castle Grayskull last night. There's an imprint of a ring pull on my forehead. Even worse than that, Joanne hasn't forgotten about the camping thing. Fuck, this might mean I actually have to go camping with her.

She bounces into the room just after I've managed to get myself into an upright position. I'm OK with standing up today as long as I can cling onto a wall.

"Rise and shine sleepyhead!"

Wait, what? I'm standing up as we speak. Does she think I'm asleep standing up?

"You're off work today right? Because we need to go score a tent."

"Score a tent?"

"I need to sit in all the tents to check their vibrations before we decide. Also I'd like a red one."

Nope, it's no use. Standing up isn't going to happen today. I flop down onto the settee. Maybe if I concentrate really hard, a shark will come along and eat me.

On top of everything else, I've now got to think of a way to get out of camping. I could kill Daniel. This is his fault. How dare he approve my idea like that.

Joanne pulls my hair. "Come on, Millets opens in half

an hour!"

Wait, that would make it… half eight? Half eight. In the morning. Doesn't she realise people can die if they do things at half eight in the morning? Going outside is out of the question.

"Fax has a vegan tent."

Maybe if I just stop breathing, everything will be OK. I have a sudden urge to listen to Metallica on full blast. This is accompanied by a vision of assorted bats and debris flying out of my head, startled by the noise.

Instead of Metallica, I'm treated to a song that I'm 99% sure Joanne is just making up as she goes along:

OHHH… *the smouldering woman is a woman that's wise,*
Come gather around, have a burger with fries,
By the tree and the stream, is where she doth plaaaaaay,
With the good fairy folk, and the man that is gay.

Go on, just stop breathing for thirty seconds. That will probably do it.

Three hours later we are in Millets. I've never set foot in a Millets before. Everything is green, including the staff. 'Green and rugged' is the best way to describe the staff and the customers. Then there's us – a walking diseased liver and a pretend vegan.

A voice in my head keeps trying to get my attention. 'Stop her, stop her now!' it's saying. I have to say something before she buys a tent. If I let her buy a tent, it's going to be that much harder to pull out of this trip. The problem is my brain is struggling to form coherent words.

One of the staff looks like Bear Grylls. She approaches us and introduces herself as Linda. Joanne demands to be shown all the red tents, and the pair of them disappear to somewhere else in the shop. There's a display tent next to me, but it's blue so Joanne has shunned it. It looks comfy. Maybe if I get inside I can say I'm testing it, and then I can have a nice sit down, just for a minute.

It's nice in here. It's better than I was expecting. It could do with a settee but still. It's not so bad lying in here.

Next thing I know Joanne's shouting me. It takes me a minute to get my bearings.

"Where are you? Look what I got!"

I now have two options:

1. Stay in this tent for the rest of my life.
2. Come out of the tent and face the fact that Joanne has managed to find and purchase a red vegan tent with positive vibrations.

I choose option 2. I chose wrong. She's holding a box. If I'm very lucky, the box will contain something better than a tent, like fifty bees.

"We're all set!"

"What did you get?"

Please say bees. Please say bees.

"It's an Avon Deluxe!"

That's probably not bees. Oh God I'm going to have to man up and tell her. The alternative is sitting in an 'Avon Deluxe' while she has sex with Fax. Oh for fuck's sake. It's not like I asked her to buy the bloody tent.

I follow her to Costa, stomach acid threatening to escape from places that aren't my stomach. She gets some fruit tea bollocks, and I get the strongest black coffee that won't immediately make me shit myself.

Right, I have to just get this over with right now. I'm sorry I let her buy a tent, but really it was her own stupid fault for throwing Skeletor out of the window. If she hadn't done that she wouldn't have been all upset and crying herself to death, and I wouldn't have had to agree to go camping. She can still use the stupid tent anyway. I don't see why I have to go with her and hold her hand and wipe her bum. The thought of wiping her bum makes me do a bit of a sick in my coffee.

Right, time to close the deal.

"Look, I have to tell you something." I take a sip of my coffee, which reminds me that I just did a bit of sick in it, which makes me want to do another load of sick. I abandon the coffee. "I'm really sorry, but there might be a money problem with this whole camping thing. I checked my balance, and I forgot about a couple of payments going out. Long story short, I don't have nearly as much cash as I thought, so I might not be able to afford camping after all." I give her my best apologetic face.

I half expect her to throw her boiling hot tea in my eyes, so I'm taken aback when she starts grinning instead.

"Well... brrrrr br br brrrrr br brr brrrrrrrrrr!"

Was that a fanfare or is she having a stroke.

"Surprise! I already paid for your ticket!"

"What?"

"Yeah, I figured I have some spare in my bank sitting around doing nothing, so I got both our tickets! I thought I'd surprise you for Christmas!"

"It's May."

"Well durr. I know – this can be your Christmas *and* birthday present! Free holiday! *And* an Avon Deluxe! Aren't I just the best buddy ever?"

I staple a grin to my face and make a mental note to kill myself later. After EastEnders. I zone out as she starts crapping on about some activity tent that's going to be there. I do catch the words 'sacred geometry in the Goddess tent', and make a mental note to kill myself even more. I want it to hurt.

When we get home Joanne shrieks and runs into the alley that separates us from next door. She comes back holding Skeletor. I guess Lidl guy didn't steal him after all. He smells of piss though, and appears to have been chewed by a baby or a large rat.

"Look! Look! He was here all along! A cat must have picked him up or something! I guess that man was picking up something else."

Well, shit.

13. JEREMY / AMELIA

"Have you never thought about what you want to do with your life?"

Karen stares at me, waiting for an answer. I don't want to have this conversation. I don't care that she's made me a coffee, that doesn't justify her acting like my dad with tits.

"I dunno. I don't really care for now. I'll just do whatever. You know, make money."

"But what do you want to *be*?"

I don't fucking know, a fucking carpet salesman. Fuck off Karen.

I shrug. I feel like everyone's telling me off recently.

"I mean look, no offence, you do a good job here. But I can't help being concerned that you're going nowhere. I mean, you work at the Co-op, and you live with that horrid hippy girl."

I should probably defend Joanne. But I'm still mad at her for tricking me into going camping.

"You can't go on coasting for the rest of your life. I know it's probably not my place, but don't you want to get married and have kids?"

I don't get this. Just because she wants to shit out a kid she assumes everyone else wants to. She can't see past her own cervix. And if you don't want to plop out a baby then you must want a high-powered career. But she means well, so I don't argue to her face.

However, my lack of response makes me look like I agree with her. It doesn't matter whether I agree with her or not, her mind's made up. Everyone should want a briefcase or a shit covered baby. I don't want either. I don't want anything really. I just want to be left alone most days.

I don't know what's got into Karen anyway. She just rocked up this morning and decided my entire existence wasn't up to scratch. And now she's stopping me doing my most fun thing, which is staring into space.

That's not to say Karen's life sounds terrible. Sometimes I'm jealous when she talks about the things she gets to do. Sometimes her husband will take her out for dinner, which sounds nice. Sometimes they go to car boot sales, where Karen will buy chairs she can hit with a hammer so they look old. Apparently that's a thing. But I don't think I'd fit in her sort of life, where you have to go round giving a shit about people all the time.

Like now, for example. Karen's giving a shit about me, and I wish she wouldn't. I wish Mr Baranski was still the manager, he never used to talk to anyone unless it was urgent. Although he did stare. And I did hear a rumour that he made models of his sister out of wood. And I never did find out what his first name was. I'm glad Karen's the manager.

"Well, I probably shouldn't talk about this, wouldn't want to jinx it..." Karen snaps me out of my coma. "... but you know as soon as I have a little one on the way I probably won't be working here any more. I want to be a full time mummy..."

I get a mental image of Karen setting up a business in her spare room where she rents out kids. I'm not sure how that would work in real life. I know they do it with dogs. I try to nod along.

"…so there'll be a manager position going. It would be some stability for you…"

Was Bananaman Eric Bana, or was that the Hulk? Eric Banana?

"…probably afford to get your own house, and not have to share with that girl. I know she smokes marijuana…"

I wonder what Karen would say if I told her Joanne pissed in my Daniel O'Donnell mug. She'd probably tut so hard her head would snap off.

"…causes paranoia. Well at least there are no little ones around. Speaking of which, I'm still having trouble deciding on names. I quite like Jeremy. For a boy, obviously, ha ha."

"Ha ha."

"Or Amelia for a girl."

Jeremy/Amelia will probably grow up to be an upstanding pillar of the community. They'll probably have a Nutri Ninja and not earn minimum wage at the Co-op. They'll probably have a fucking horse, that's how successful they'll be. I wish I was drunk.

Karen leaves not long after this, thank God. I know she means well, but I have more pressing problems than what I want to do with my life. I need to get out of this camping thing, but it's looking more and more unlikely. My brain is refusing to do its job and come up with an excuse. I don't know what I pay it for.

When half 10 rolls around I close up then hang round sorting the magazines in alphabetical order. I don't want to go home. I feel like I can't go home until I've thought of a rock-solid reason to not go camping, one that won't mean Joanne will lie on the floor crying again. I try not to acknowledge that Karen thinks my life's a failure.

I needn't have worried about going home – there are two voices in the living room and it stinks of weed so she's occupied. There's a man's voice – oh my God is it? Is it Fax? Oh, it's just Spoz.

Spoz has never done anything wrong to me but I don't like him for several reasons. Firstly, Spoz is not a proper name. Why is he called Spoz? Is it short for something? Sponald? The whole sound of it makes me think of 80s psychos with bomber jackets and safety pins through their noses. It just grates on me. Secondly, he has a bright pink mohican. This makes me think of 80s psychos even more. Being around Spoz is like watching an episode of *Grange Hill*, if everyone on *Grange Hill* killed each other all the time. Like I say, not his fault, but I'm not a fan of spending much time around him. Joanne knows this, so it's a perfect excuse to go straight to bed without discussing camping, Fax, or Fax's burning desire to do it under a rowan tree.

14. TROLLEY

I wake up in the biggest panic of my life. My brain has chosen now to remember that today I have to go to my cousin's wedding. This is the very last thing I ever want to do.

My cousin Laura is some big bollocks superstar in our family because she was on an episode of *Say Yes To The Dress*. She went to some wedding shop in London and tried on some dresses, and they filmed it for TV. In the episode she was saying things like "Oh I don't know, this lace doesn't quite match my vision." I do not get on with Laura. Also, she's consistently the most orange person I know.

I lie there and consider not going. I know Laura won't really give a shit if I go or not. In fact, she'd probably love it, because A) I wouldn't be there, and B) then she can bitch to everyone about how horrible I am for not turning up, then she can do fake crying and everyone will say how brave and nice she is.

This scenario enrages me, so I decide to go to the wedding just to spite her.

Two hours later I am on the train to Nottingham. The train smells of piss and Ginsters. I am wearing the one dress I own for emergencies.

"Trolley."

The man is pushing the food and drink trolley down the aisle.

"Trolley."

Why does he keep saying that? Does he think we can't see the fucking trolley?

He stops at me.

"Trolley?"

I'm tempted to say 'trolley' back to him to see what he does, but instead I find myself saying "Two of your miniature Smirnoffs please. And an Um Bongo."

I pay him and he wanders off, blurting out "trolley" every three seconds.

I put the Um Bongo in my bag for later and neck a vodka. A load of guys start laughing at the end of the carriage. I wonder if it's a stag do? Is some other poor fucker getting married? Did his fiancée go on *Say Yes To The Dress*? I wonder if he's anything like Robbie, the guy who's marrying Laura. I met him once, at a Toby Carvery. He nodded for an hour, in between going to get Laura's drinks for her. I wonder if he's going to just nod through the vows.

I wouldn't blame him. You don't argue with my cow of a cousin. I learned that the hard way when I was eleven. I told her that her jelly shoes were stupid and crap, and she retaliated by telling my mum I'd said she should have been aborted.

After that it was just polite conversation at family parties, and the odd 'like' on Facebook. Even that got me into trouble. She once wrote a huge passive aggressive Facebook post about how she thought she looked really fat, and I 'liked' it. I had an angry phone call from my mum the next day, accusing me of 'fat shaming'.

Oh shit. Shit shit shit. I forgot to get a present. Fuck. Anything would have done, I'd have just wrapped up the sodding remote control for the TV if only I'd remembered. Oh fuck, now I'm going to have to stop at a shop. And I refuse to spend more than, I don't know, nine quid. What shops do they have in Nottingham train station? I run through the likelihood of leaving before they open their presents. That seems doable, so I'll just buy them whatever. It won't matter.

Nottingham station contains a Greggs, a WH Smith, and a Boots that's shut. A sausage roll is probably out of the question, although I'd be happy if someone bought me a sausage roll. WH Smith it is. I toy with the idea of buying them a stack of porn mags, but she'd definitely have a meltdown on Facebook about that, which I then wouldn't be able to not 'like'.

A ha – three autobiographies for a tenner. Perfect. I choose the three thickest ones, because that will make the largest possible present once it's wrapped. I'd always wondered why WH Smith kept going – now I know. I buy autobiographies of David Davis, Ben Fogle and Sean Connery, and some wrapping paper. It's a bit over my nine quid limit, but I think it does the job pretty well.

15. WEDDING

I get a taxi to the wedding venue – some bullshit hotel. She's paid someone to put crepe paper on all the chairs. I do the obligatory 'Oh look it's you, you're still alive, seeing you again is the most thrilling experience of my life' stuff, but only for a minute because I've arrived just before kick-off.

Laura smarms up the aisle while I sing 'here comes the bride, short fat and fucking orange' in my head, some sniffing and nodding goes on, then it's over and it's time to go stand at the bar and avoid people.

My mum and dad are the first people to stop me avoiding them. "We didn't think you were going to make it, you never RSVP'd!" My mum gives me a hug that stinks of Cerruti 1881, then immediately tuts. "You haven't been drinking already?"

"No it's from last night," I say, making the situation ten times worse. "Anyway, Laura looks… you can't miss her."

My dad jostles over and gives me an identical hug, only this time it smells of Lynx Africa. "And where's your date?"

Oh shit. I'd been so busy thinking about buying the present and not dying, I'd completely forgotten you're supposed to bring someone else to a wedding. If only I'd been nicer to trolley guy, maybe he could have come with me.

"Oh, well, no it's just me."

He hesitates for a second. "Oh, no Joanne then?"

Why on fucking Earth would I bring Joanne here.

"No, I don't think Joanne was invited was she?"

He's suddenly fascinated by something in the far corner of the room. "Oh well, very modern and all that. Independent woman!"

My dad definitely has been drinking. He can't have had that many because they're on in a bit.

My parents are a semi-retired club duo. You can tell this by looking at them. No one ever asks 'What do you do?' when they meet my parents, because they know. Only club singers have that particular brand of grey mullet/sequinned jacket/cheated by life expression combo. They introduce themselves at their gigs by saying the following:

"I'm Shelia…"

"…and I'm Pete…"

"AND TOGETHER WE ARE… SAFARI!"

They say this last bit together because they think it sounds really professional. Then they sing 60s and 70s music for an hour while old people sit there waiting for the bingo to come on.

I used to love going to their gigs when I was a kid. I got to stay up past midnight, which was the most dangerous and badass thing in the world. And to a kid it was a massive, glamorous night out.

We'd get to a gig and they'd start setting the gear up while I wandered off to explore the place. Sometimes I got lucky and found an arcade machine, and then I was all set. While they were doing their thing, I'd spend the evening playing Space Invaders or Pac Land, standing on a milk crate so I could reach the buttons.

If there was no game, my parents would placate me

with Panda Pops and bags of bar snacks – scampi fries, cheese moments – and I'd sit at the table stuffing my face and feeling very grown up. If I was really good they'd buy me a bingo ticket, which I'd then sit and scribble all over because I was a small child.

I think they've always been a bit disappointed that I never wanted to 'follow in their footsteps'. They don't seem to care that I can't sing or dance or anything like that. Occasionally they'll ask me if I want them to set up an audition with their agent – a man called Gordon who calls them 'artistes' and does his business from a pub. I always decline.

It goes without saying that they are the entertainment for the wedding. They would have been offended beyond repair had Laura booked anyone else.

They get on the stage and start doing their 'set', which I must have heard a thousand times before. Laura is standing at the main table being orange. People are congratulating her, presumably on getting married and not on being orange. She looks over at the bar and sees me with my free drinks lined up next to me. I wave at her. She looks at me like someone just slapped her in the face with someone else's penis. I'm glad I bought her three autobiographies.

When Laura and Robbie get up for their first dance, I fight the urge to stand up and boo them. Instead I concentrate on a woman in the crowd who I don't know. She is, for whatever reason, clapping along to Leona Lewis' 'A Moment Like This'. Some other romantic shit happens, then mercifully it's nearly time to be getting back for my train.

My dad comes to say goodbye. My mum's somewhere in a corner with my other relations. My dad's very pissed.

"I'm sorry Joanne couldn't be here." He pauses for a

second. "You know… you could have brought her, your mum and me would have had no problem with it…"

I'm surprised he even remembers Joanne. They've only met her twice, and I don't remember her doing anything particularly mental.

"… I'm a man of the world. I mean, as long as you're happy…"

"…"

"…"

Oh my fucking god. Oh fucking Jesus Christ and Satan and Alan Sugar. Fucking fuck.

The following things occur to me:

1. Despite having had several boyfriends, my dad now thinks I've decided to become a lesbian.
2. He also thinks that the lesbian me would choose Joanne as my girlfriend. On purpose.
3. My mum's hiding and she's made him come and have this talk with me.
4. I spend far too much time wishing I was dead recently.

"I'm not… me and Joanne aren't…"

His face immediately turns hotter than the sun. "Oh, righty dokey. Sorry, me and your mum thought…"

Oh Christ.

"We thought you'd decided to…"

Decided? How does someone decide to become a lesbian?

This new, heady mix of embarrassment and cocktails has left me wanting to do a sick all over my dad. To distract myself I start gathering my things ready to leave. My dad takes this to mean he's shamed me into leaving a wedding I was otherwise enjoying. That is not what this is.

"…It's just that, you know, she has those hairy armpits…"

"She does that sometimes, but that's nothing to do

with me. God, honestly, you've got it completely wrong."

"I'm so sorry."

"Honestly it's fine." All my stuff fit in my handbag earlier, why won't it now? "It's fine, I'm fine. I have to catch my train though."

"Oh, you aren't stopping? They're just about to open the presents I think. Me and your mum got them a Nespresso."

They've never bought me a fucking Nespresso.

"Sorry I really have to go. It's the last train back. You guys were really good –"

"– If you stay we're going to do 'Wig Wam Bam', you used to love dancing to that…"

"Sorry, it really is the last train and I'll miss it. I'll ring you in the week OK?"

I give him a hug and leave him to break the news to my mum that I'm not a lesbian, just a failure. There's no fucking way I'm sticking around to watch Laura open the autobiographies. I'm sure I'll read about it on Facebook.

16. STAG DO

At the train station there are five men dressed as Power Rangers. There are two blue ones, two green ones and a red one, I assume because none of them wanted to be the girl ones. I thought there were more men colours than that though? One of the green ones approaches me for a high five.

"Woooo! I'm getting married!"

I want to ask him what he'd think if he got three auto-biographies as a wedding present. I wonder if these are the laughing guys from the earlier train.

Green demands to have a selfie taken with me. Then one of the blue ones falls on his face. "I've broken my cock!" he shouts. Green is too busy with his phone to help Blue, and the others are too busy trying open beer bottles with their teeth.

This reminds me that I've got a vodka and an Um Bongo in my bag. The vodka will probably go off first, so I'd better drink that now. My miniature bottle is greeted with a cheer from the Power Rangers. Blue is still on the floor.

"I've been to a wedding," I say by way of explanation. I don't add 'and I hate my life and my dad just ordered me to imagine shagging Joanne'.

"I'm getting married!" says Green. I'm touched that he thinks I give a shit. He produces a beer bottle from nowhere that I can see and plops down next to me. He does a 'cheers' with my bottle. Blue is still on the floor.

I think I'm supposed to say something to Green. I might as well say something interesting. "I went to my cousin's wedding. At the wedding my dad accused me of being a lesbian. Now I'm on my way home."

Green thinks this is hilarious, and beckons the others over so I can tell them my fascinating anecdote. I can't imagine how their evening's been if this is the highlight of it.

"Are you a lesbian like?"

"No, I'm just single."

These guys clearly aren't single, because instead of immediately trying to crack on to me, they decide to take me under their wing. "Come and be a stag for the night love."

I make a deal with myself. If Blue gets up in the next five minutes and isn't dead, I'll go with them.

"My cock! Someone help me with my cock!"

I guess I'm a stag.

We board the train and they start singing some song they know but I don't. I catch the line 'scrotum army'. My head's starting to feel like it might fall off my body.

40 minutes and two bottles of beer later, we stagger into Wetherspoons. They're still singing the scrotum army song until the manager asks them to stop because "this establishment doesn't hold a music license".

We all congratulate the groom-to-be about seventeen times. There's talk of curry. There's talk of Blue going to hospital to have his cock seen to. There's talk about how it's a shame I'm single, because I have "smashing tits".

The rest of the night blurs into a montage of shots and kissing a guy who I think is called Eric. I have no idea how I get home but I do. Joanne is still up. She's doing her rage yoga again, but I don't think I have the co-ordination to kick her over this time.

"Twatting fuck! Oh, where have you been? I was getting a bit worried."

I remember Joanne was still in bed when I left, so she wouldn't know where I've been. "I went to my cousin's wedding, then I went to a stag do." I fall over a bit at this point.

"They had the stag do after the wedding?"

"No, it was a different stag do. A different people."

Thanks to her yoga she's too serene to bother questioning me about that. "Was the wedding nice?"

"No. It was Laura."

"Oh."

"I bought them some books."

"Books? Did they like them?"

"I hope not."

I don't tell her my dad thought we were a couple, and she doesn't ask me anything else. She's too in the zone, what with calling the living room floor a cunt. I go to bed.

17. FEET OF LEAVES

It's settled. I'm going to this stupid festival with Joanne. I haven't been able to think of a reason not to go, and now it's five days away. Joanne is Skyping with Fax non-stop. His hair is longer than it was in the photo I saw of him.

I try not to be around when they're Skyping, because they do things like chant together. And he plays her songs he's written on his acoustic guitar.

Last night they had the following conversation:

Fax: "I've always had an affinity with dragons."

Joanne: "You're so viral." (I think she meant virile).

Fax: "Of course, humans just don't understand when you're an other being. They can't see past the human realm."

Joanne: "That's so sad."

Fax: I don't mind about them, I know you understand me. I know you're a fellow spirit traveller."

Joanne: "Not dragons though. I've always been a wood nymph."

Fax: "That's exactly you. The way your feet glide across the forest floor."

Joanne: (giggles)

Fax: "I wrote you another song today."

Joanne: (squeals) "Yay your songs are so beautiful."
All this while I was trying to watch the news.
Joanne: "Will you play it for me now?"
Fax: "I will for you, m'lady."

I gave up on *Midlands Today*, because we were then treated to Fax's song, which consisted of a tune I'm sure was nicked from the Beatles, and was called 'Feet Of Leaves'.

Fax: "Ohhh..."
Why do all their songs start with 'Ohhh'?
Fax: "In the bright forest dell, where the wood elves do play,
They gather around in the warm sun of day,
To see their beautiful queeeeeeeeen
As she dances yonder,
Her magical footsteps enchanting and pure,
The leaves they do fall, and the footsteps do dance..."
I left the room at that point.

I'm trying to leave my packing until the last possible minute, in case I happen to get enough cyanide to fill my suitcase. I also haven't tried to get time off work yet. It's one thing that I've agreed to go, but I'm not losing my job over it.

I'm not sure what you need for a long weekend in a tent surrounded by hippies. Probably a weapon of some sort. Clothes and shit. This puts a terrifying thought in my mind that it might be a nudist thing. I briefly consider packing all the clothes I own, then I can wear them all at once if the nudist thing becomes an issue. It's probably not going to come to that. After all, I'll have my weapon.

Joanne keeps talking at me about what crystals to pack. "Rose quartz carries amazing love energy, but I don't want to appear too forward with Fax."

I don't think she needs to worry about appearing 'too

forward'. The guy's already been talking about organic lube.

Jesus, I need to tell her I might not be able to get time off work. The stress is making me constipated. I'm dying to sit and have a nice poo while reading a *Beano* annual but I can't. I blame Joanne for this. Because of her restless loins I've got one more problem than I should have.

Well I've got four hours to figure something out. I need to either get time off today or tell her I'm definitely not going.

"So how did you get time off for this? What did you tell your boss?"

Shit. A) She seems to be able to teleport into a room at will and B) She can now read my mind. This is a worrying development. I really need to sort out some weapons. We've got a spatula somewhere that's got quite a sharp corner on it.

Oh God, I might as well tell her now. You never know, she might be able to use some crystals to magic me some time off.

"I... haven't actually got any time off yet. I was coming to that."

"What? How could you not have time off! Doesn't she know you're going on holiday?"

This is not a holiday. Not for me. What do I say? That in the back of my mind I guess I was hoping Joanne would suddenly die so I wouldn't have to go?

"Well... it's hard at the moment. It's alright for you, you don't work proper hours."

"I completely do! I have to work when the vibrations are aligned, not just when I feel like it!"

It's probably best to say nothing to this.

"Don't you have any holidays left?"

Her skirt has started whirling. That means she's properly annoyed. I don't like this, it means she might start pissing in my things again. A thought crosses my mind – does she wear those floaty skirts so she has easy access for pissing in my things?

"I might have a couple… I'm sorry, I guess I just didn't think about it."

She stops mid whirl to have a think. "That's OK, you can always be ill. What do you normally say when you need to pull a sickie?"

I think back to when I last phoned in sick. I can barely remember it. Something about my phone being in French? That probably won't work this time. Oh that was it – I had an Uncle Jeff with leprosy. Jesus, Karen can't possibly have believed that.

I tell Joanne about Uncle Jeff. To my surprise she doesn't immediately burst out laughing.

"That's brilliant! Just tell her he died!"

She has no respect for my poor fake relatives.

"So you want me to tell my boss that my fake Uncle Jeff died of leprosy?"

"Yes please."

"And what if she doesn't believe me?"

"Why wouldn't she believe you? She'd have to be very hard-hearted to not give you time off for a funeral."

"Yes but this 'funeral' would apparently last four days."

"They do that in Greece I think."

"Right. So let's recap. You want me to tell my boss that, not only has my fake Uncle Jeff died of leprosy, but also that I've decided to become Greek."

"Maybe not decided, but maybe you've just found out you are Greek."

"What, and I just found this out this week?"

"Yes."

I start to argue with her some more, but her phone

rings. No doubt it's Fax calling to tell her she has spiritual feet. She buggers off, leaving me to sit there ignoring my packing again.

18. UNCLE JEFF, PART 2

Work drags, as usual. As much as I don't want to go to this lentil festival, some time off work would be nice. I spend the first part of my shift dithering and eating peanuts.

I don't want Karen to get here, because I still haven't figured out how to approach my fake bereavement. The minute she gets in I'm going to have to put on a sad face. It's fucking hard though, every time I try to do a sad face I start laughing. It's a good job I'm not really going to a funeral.

Maybe I should try thinking about sad things? Let's see:
- My life
- Poor starving orphans
- That time I accidentally trod on a worm

None of these are hitting the right note. I'm getting desperate. Why can't I just man up and do the sensible thing, which is to just not turn up to work for four days? That would give me plenty of time to think of an excuse. I could put a bandage round my head and tell Karen I fell off a cliff and have spent four days climbing back up the cliff.

I'm going to chicken out, I'm no good at this sort of thing. I wonder if I can somehow manage to be at work, and at this festival? If I had a car I could drive there and back between customers if I drove really fast.

Once again I find myself furious at Joanne. To calm myself down I open a packet of sherbet and eat it. I don't want to eat the liquorice stick thing, so I hide it in the till.

Fuck this, I'm not fucking going. Am I really going to risk my job just because Joanne wants me to hold her hand on a date? This is stupid.

And I know what will happen. The minute we get there she'll meet Fax and she'll be off. I'll be left to sod about and fend for myself with a bunch of vegans. I might feel differently if we were going somewhere good, but we're not. My mind's made up now. If she needs me that fucking much she can bring Fax to the Co-op for four days.

"Hi love, are you OK?"

Fuck. I need to start paying attention. How long has Karen been standing there? I hope I don't have all sherbet around my face.

Speaking of faces, Karen's face is all concerned. Clearly I've had a stroke or something and not realised.

"How are you doing?"

"Oh, you know…"

She's hovering round me like an ovulating bee. I'm starting to think something is actually wrong. She did see me with the sherbet and now she wants to discuss my 'problem'.

"I'm sorry, I heard about your uncle."

Oh well this is an unexpected twist.

"Joanne phoned me and let me know. You know, I sometimes don't have a lot of time for that girl, but that was thoughtful of her."

I have a horrible urge to burst out laughing, more from not knowing what else to do than anything. I'm starting to grasp that Joanne has involved me in some sort of lie, and that I now have to go along with it. Given what we talked about earlier, I assume my poor Uncle Jeff is no more. And how did Joanne get Karen's number? She must have been through my phone. Mental note to become angry about that as soon as I stop being confused.

The gods are smiling on me, because a customer chooses this moment to pay for her *Guardian*. Karen busies herself with checking the milk.

"£1.80, ta."

The woman looks at me and starts sucking her teeth. "Let's try that again shall we?"

"Sorry?"

"I *said*, let's try that again, shall we?"

This woman's a serial killer. They don't normally wear cardigans. I hope Karen witnesses my murder and isn't too focused on rearranging the milk.

"Erm… £1.80?"

"I *think* you mean 'That will be £1.80 *please, Madam*'. Honestly, shop assistants don't seem to be able to grasp the most *basic* words."

I look at her. She starts poking her finger at me.

"I think it benefits us all, even your types, to remember to use manners. Especially since I'm spending money and therefore paying your wage. You should be thankful."

'My types'? What? She wants me to beg her to pay the money for something she wants to buy? My brain's struggling with this. What did she mean 'my types'? Right this woman's saying nonsense and I need to get rid of her.

"Look do you want your stupid paper or not?"

She reacts as if I've just threatened to bum her to death with a fish finger. I hate it when people fake heart attacks.

"WHERE IS YOUR MANAGER!"

"Hi, what seems to be the problem?"

Ha. Karen snuck up behind the old bitch and made her shit herself. Good.

"Your *worker* has just been unbelievably rude to me!"

Karen keeps her voice pleasant. "Was this before or after you were rude to her?"

"What? I… I did no such thing!"

"Yes you did and I saw you pointing in her face. It's rude to point."

Karen's using the tone she'll use with her kids when she finally gets to have some. I sort of wish Karen was my mum.

"I cannot tolerate my staff being verbally abused. I'm afraid I'm going to have to ask you to leave."

I can't help myself, I have to butt in. "Wow," I say to the woman. "Imagine getting thrown out of the *Co-op.* That must be so embarrassing."

Karen gives me a look.

"I have never been so insulted in all my life!"

Saying 'calm your tits love' to this woman probably isn't going to help, so I don't do that.

"I shall be sure to see my circle of friends never shop here again! My husband is on the council!"

Karen sighs. "That's nice for you. Now if you wouldn't mind leaving, you're causing a disturbance and I will have to call the police."

This is a lie. We're the only ones in here.

"I am writing to your head office!" With that parting shot she flounces out. The stupid bitch is probably going to go to London and try to buy a *Guardian* from Harrods.

As soon as the woman's out of earshot, Karen says "It's OK, I heard everything she said to you. I was about to come over. God, where's Nick when you need him?"

"I know," I say. "Nutters don't only come in in the evenings."

Karen picks the paper up to put it back. "Anyway, I'm sorry you had to deal with that. Today of all days. I'm actually very grateful you managed to show up today. Joanne said she didn't really think you were up to it but that you didn't want to let me down. It's appreciated."

She pats my hand. I can't stop thinking about the liquorice I hid in the till.

"I know you don't want me to keep talking about it, so I'll just tell you that of course time off isn't a problem. Joanne said you might need to go help with the arrangements?"

"Oh, yeah. Arranging and stuff."

She assumes my confusion and general lack of detail is because *Guardian* bitch just traumatised me. I'll run with that.

"I phoned Kay, and she said she doesn't mind covering for a few days. In fact she said she'd be glad of the extra money so you mustn't think you're putting us out in any way. If you can get through your shift today, we can work it so you don't have to be back in until next Tuesday."

This is really awkward. "OK, thanks."

She's still fiddling with the *Guardian*. "I'm afraid I don't really know anything about Greek Orthodox funerals. They sound like they involve a lot of planning though. Anyway, you don't want me harping on about it. Just to put your mind at rest that your cover is all arranged."

I can't believe Joanne is such an evil genius. I've underestimated her.

19. BUS

Joanne has booked us seats on a female-only minibus. She occasionally does things with a group called 'Goddess Empowerment'. This group has paid for the minibus, and it stinks of lavender and sweat.

It's OK, I'm prepared for being trapped in a metal box with a dozen people who are the opposite of me. Since I'm technically going on holiday, I've packed exotic booze: ouzo and Pernod. Sadly these are in my suitcase, so I'll have to make do with one of the gin miniatures that are clinking in my handbag.

Joanne had a go at me when she saw me packing my suitcase:

"You can't take that!"

"Why not?"

"A suitcase isn't a festival thing. You need a rucksack."

"I don't have a rucksack so tough shit."

"God why do you even need a suitcase? You don't need to bring much."

Wrong. I need to bring the contents of Bargain Booze.

"You just need, like, a few tops."

At least she didn't see me packing my spatula.

"Well unless you want to carry all my stuff, I'm taking

my suitcase."

I still don't know why she was so offended about the suitcase. It's probably some weird thing about me showing her up and looking like a capitalist. I don't know.

I open a tiny bottle of Gordon's. A woman immediately pipes up behind me –

"I can smell alcohol Titania, can you smell alcohol?"

I can't decide if Titania's friend sounds disapproving or hopeful.

Loud sniff. "Yes, I can smell it too! This is unacceptable."

I neck my gin before it kicks off. I don't look at Joanne but I know she's trying to kill me with her mind. I don't care.

There's a tap on my shoulder. "Excuse me, I think you'll find there is a 'no alcohol' rule on this bus. This is for everyone's safety, so would you mind not drinking alcohol please."

Objectively speaking, I suppose she was pretty polite about it. However, I am not objective, so I turn round in my seat to face them.

"Is that a real rule? Only I'm not actually doing anything wrong. It's not actually affecting you personally is it?"

I carry on before she can reply. "Of course, if you're allergic to alcohol fumes and can prove that, then of course I'll stop. Or if you can show me an official list of 'rules'. Otherwise, maybe you're just fibbing."

Joanne intervenes. "Sorry, of course she'll put it away. She's been under a lot of stress lately, she didn't mean anything by it."

I'm only 'under a lot of stress' because these grass eating harpies are trying to stop me drinking. I'm dying to blurt out that I wouldn't have to drink on the bus if they didn't all stink.

"Oh the fumes are making my gluten intolerance flare up," wails Titania's friend.

"Don't worry, she's putting it away now," says Titania.

This has become a matter of principle. "I'm doing no such thing," I say, getting a mini Bell's out of my bag. Joanne snatches it from me while Titania tells me off. I hear the words 'unbelievably insensitive' and 'borderline misogynistic'.

I don't speak to Joanne for the rest of the journey. Joanne doesn't speak to me for the rest of the journey. A group of women start singing a song about mountains being female. I could bear this if it weren't for them all lifting their arms for the chorus. Every time they get to the chorus I hold my breath and pray the bus will crash.

Joanne has made friends with Titania and her friend, the fucking Judas. She's leaning over her seat, talking to them about tarot cards.

"Of course, the Queen of Cups is the most empowering. If I don't draw it first time then I know my energies aren't aligned properly, so I deal again until I sense they're in tune."

"I use the Gardnerian Lightworker deck."

"Patchouli oil helps to focus the energies."

"There's a tarot workshop in the Aphrodite Tent."

When Joanne first asked me to go to this festival, she tried to fob me off with some bollocks about it being a 'folk festival'. It's no such thing. In fact, the thing she's dragging me to is a 'new age' festival, which is the worst thing in the world. Joanne knows how I feel about things like this, which is why she never specifically mentioned the 'new age' part. And now I'm trapped, hurtling towards Wales, where I will be forced to spend the next four days surrounded by 'lightworkers'.

It's drizzling when the bus finally stops, but I will happily be naked in a typhoon just to escape these women and their armpits and their 'gluten intolerance'.

We get our luggage and trudge through the rain to where some people are milling around. I assume this is the entrance. Someone is sitting against a fence playing a lute. I want to kill him.

I can't help it, my brain starts to think about all the other things I could be doing right now:

- Lying in a hot bath
- Drinking wine and eating doughnuts
- Watching *The Walking Dead*
- Anything

My brain clearly hates me. 'Look what you've done,' it's saying. 'You've dragged us into this and now we both have to suffer, so thank you very fucking much.' I apologise to my brain, and let it know I would welcome it switching off for the duration.

Snippets from the queue:

"If all women let their body hair grow naturally, society would have no choice but to accept it."

"Actually, I find fresh lavender to be much less harsh than commercial soap."

"There was a man in the queue last week who objected to my needing to go in front of him. He was a terrible racist."

"I'm particularly looking forward to hearing Jane Ilfracombe's multi-gender poetry."

My feet start subconsciously grinding into the rapidly emerging mud. I think they're trying to tunnel me to Australia. I welcome this effort.

Three years later we get to the check-in bit. There's a sign stapled to a post:

This is a tolerant safe space, so please do not use words that relate to someone's ethnic or cultural background, or words that refer to their gender or sexuality.

No one should have to use these words anyway! We're all here to have fun! Think before you speak!

After reading this, my game plan is to lock myself in the tent and not say anything to anyone until it's time to go home. I turn to say something to Joanne, but she's disappeared. The stupid turncoat bitch has probably gone off with Titania and her friend. I hope their tent isn't near our tent. I'd hate to kill Titania's friend with one of my fumes.

Speaking of tents, I should probably find Joanne because she has our 'Avon Deluxe'. I scan the crowd but all I can see is hundreds of people wearing brightly coloured wool. Panic sets in, possibly helped by the gin.

"JOANNE!"

People turn round to look at me. I look round too; hopefully they'll think someone else shouted. I hear Joanne shouting back from somewhere.

"WHAT!"

I still can't see her. If that guy doesn't stop playing that lute I will smash it over his head. That's apparently within the rules as long as I don't call him gay.

"WHERE ARE YOU JOANNE?"

"HERE!"

Fucking brilliant. But before I can kill myself, I see Joanne shuffling towards me. She knocks someone over with the tent without noticing. This makes me decide to forgive her. That and the fact that she has my house on her back.

She looks ecstatic. She looks like she's finally found her 'people'. I suppose she has. She runs over and hugs me, our gin related spat forgotten –

"Ohmygodthisisbrill…"

She has mud on her face, and we haven't even been here half an hour. I don't know where she went, but I don't think she's found Fax yet or she'd have been shagging him in a corner by now.

Right, I've had enough of this festival. I'm going to go sit in the corner with my booze and wait for Joanne to sort our tickets out.

"Right, you stand in the queue, I'm off. Come and find me when we're sorted."

Before she can reply I take my suitcase and head off towards the first relatively quiet spot I can find, which is next to a bin. If I try really hard, I can block out all the hippies that are giving me looks because of my suitcase. What is it with my suitcase? Is it a symbol of capitalist oppression or something? No one told me. To be fair, Joanne sort of did, but she doesn't count because she's mental and I wasn't listening.

I'm probably in for a bit of a wait so I'd better get sorted out. I open my horrible capitalist suitcase and rummage around. Thank God, Daniel is safe and sound. I wrapped him in a pair of knickers.

"Sorry Daniel, I didn't want you to get all broken. Shall we have a drink?"

I think Daniel's a bit shy, because he just gives me a kind of 'do what you want' look. Well I will. But I feel a bit too self-conscious to crack open a huge bottle of ouzo, so I just get one of my miniatures out of my handbag. Thankfully no one starts saying a list of made up rules at me.

Once I've had a few glugs of vodka, I start to relax. Maybe this won't be so bad after all. I mean, it is sort of a free holiday. I should probably stop being such a Negative

Nancy. 'That's the spirit', says Daniel.

A man sits down next to me and starts playing the bongos. Daniel is fucking wrong and a bellend.

20. SMOULDERING WOMAN

This is bullshit. We've only been here an hour and already I want to kill every vegan I've ever seen. Which was only about three until I came here, and now the running total is 70,000.

Joanne got our tickets then dragged me into the next field, and then across some more fields, and now we're sitting around in a spot she's found that she's decided is 'aligned' correctly. Both of us are realising that we have no idea how to put up a tent, much less the complicated sounding 'Avon Deluxe'.

Joanne's in a mood because I'm refusing to get the tent out and put it up all by myself while she fucks off looking for Fax. She doesn't want to start getting the tent out and neither do I, so we've reached a compromise – the tent is still in its box and we're both going to sit here until we die.

On top of this, Joanne is having a meltdown because she can't get a signal on her phone, and she thinks Fax won't be able to get in touch with her. I'd assumed they were going to use some telepathy bollocks to communicate, like whales and vulcans do.

A thought occurs. "Maybe Fax can help us with the tent when we find him?"

Instead of cheering up, Joanne starts crying. Well, not crying exactly, but a strange noise is coming from her. She punches herself in the head.

"I'll never find him! You won't help me put the tent up and I've lost Fax!"

I feel bad for her. Not bad enough to do anything to help, but it's getting close. Joanne is now doing breathing exercises, which is better than her weird fake crying.

"I need to centre myself. I need to borrow your coat."

"My coat? What for?"

"I just told you, I need to centre myself. Give me your coat to lie on."

I've got no idea where she's going with this, but I do know she's not having my coat. Given the mud, it would go from black to brown in seconds. And anyway it's in my suitcase.

Before I can start arguing with her over this, she's opening the tent box and pulling stuff out of it. She pulls out the groundsheet and spreads it out on the floor. Just when I think she's finally being proactive and starting to sort the tent out, she leaves the rest of the tent where it is and les face down on the sheet.

Oh for fuck's sake, she's being a dead fish again. People are looking.

It's time for another drink. I'm down to one whiskey miniature, then I'll have to crack open my suitcase stash. I find myself being a bit furtive while opening the whiskey; I'm half expecting Titania's friend to appear and start being diabetic.

This is terrible. Everyone's looking at us, wondering why we're not putting up our tent and why Joanne's dead. I should at least have a go at getting the stuff out of the box. We can probably figure it out between us. It occurs to me that if we don't put the tent up, we'll have nowhere to live for the next four days.

I'm torn between trying to sort the tent out myself and beating Joanne to death with my suitcase. I abandon the suitcase idea because my suitcase is full of breakable bottles. I settle for kicking her up the arse.

"Come on, we need to get this tent sorted out. Imagine if we leave it till it's dark, that's gonna be ten times worse."

"befnnfiueyxnwdgefg…"

"Yes I know. OK, once we get the tent put up I'll come and help you find Fax."

I resent the fact that I'm having to plead with her to put up her own fucking tent, at a festival I never wanted to come to. But clouds are starting to form and whatever pathetic survival instinct I've got is kicking in. It's time to be practical; there's plenty of time after this to get hammered and pass out until it's time to go home.

Just when I'm starting to think this is a losing battle, the thought of finding Fax and doing a mind meld with him prompts Joanne to get up off the floor. At least we've already got the groundsheet down. Joanne empties the box of tent bits on the floor.

"Have you ever put a tent up before?"

I can't believe she's asking me this. I've told her a dozen times that I hate camping. She better not be relying on me to put this bastard up.

"No I haven't, but it's OK because you've done it loads of times haven't you?"

No reply.

"Haven't you?"

"God chill out it's not gonna be that hard! It's only sticks and a blanket."

I suspect she's wrong.

21. NEIGHBOURS

We're sitting on the floor sobbing. Ten minutes ago Joanne got annoyed and just stuck all the poles together, so now we've got one long pole and a pile of bits. This didn't help. Joanne is sobbing because she can't go find Fax until the tent is up; I'm sobbing because I'm not in a coma.

To make matters worse, the man with the lute is now our neighbour. He's currently trying to play 'Greensleeves', but one of his strings has snapped and he can't do any high bits. Occasionally he'll try to sing the high notes instead. Since he hasn't once offered to help us with our tent, I think I'm well within my rights to go set fire to his lute. Even Joanne is losing the will to live now.

"Fax will think I don't love him!"

I don't reply, because I can't decide if she's genuinely heartbroken, or if she's trying to get out of putting the tent up. I doubt Fax will run off and leave if he hasn't met up with Joanne in the first hour.

"What if he meets someone else while I'm stuck here? These are so many floaty goddesses here!"

I look around. I can see fat women in jumpers and men with stupid hair. No goddesses. I bet they can all put tents up though. But that shouldn't be enough to lure Fax away, not from what I've seen on Skype. Anyway, I still think she's just trying to get out of putting the tent up.

I'm getting a bit sick of sitting around in the mud, so I undo the pole and start trying to seriously figure out where each bit goes. There's a set of instructions, but they're either in Swedish or I can't read them properly because I've drunk all my miniatures. But I do get the following things:

"Assemble the three shock-corded tent poles. Carefully seat each section."

"Insert the post end of the pole into its grommet on the corner stake-out web."

"The vestibule door of the fly can be rolled up at the bottom."

What is any of this. Oh God we're homeless for four days. We'll have to sleep in a tree.

No, bullshit. We can do this. "Come on Jo, we need to seriously sort this out." I know what a pole is, so we can start from there. I also know what a tent is, and I'm fully confident I can figure out which bit is the bottom.

Joanne's staring at her phone as if she can magic a signal. Maybe she can, or more likely she thinks she can magic me to do everything while she fucking sits there.

"I'M GOING TO KICK YOU IN THE FACE JOANNE."

Our neighbour stops playing his lute. Good.

"JOANNE!"

"Fine! God!" Joanne hauls herself off the floor and drags her carcass over to me. She picks up what I think is a shock-corded tent pole. "Where does this bit go?"

You know what, scrap that earlier threat. I'm going to kick myself in the face instead.

"For fuck's sake Joanne you bought this bloody tent, why don't you know how to put it up?"

"Chill out! It's not gonna be that hard."

"You don't even know where the pole goes!"

"You need to chill out, seriously."

Considering she was lying face down on the floor in a pit of despair a minute ago, this is fucking rich coming from her."

OK, sensible head on. Oh God I need a drink. We can figure this out, we'll have to.

"OK, you read the instructions out to me, and I'll try to fit the bits together."

Joanne peers at the instructions –

"Important – we advise you to assemble your Avon Deluxe at least once before you go camping to become familiar with the assembly of the tent…"

A bad thing happens then. The short version is that we end up with one shock-corded tent pole less than we need, after I spend five minutes trying to hit Joanne with it, failing to hit Joanne, and snapping it on the ground instead.

Shit.

Lute man is now hiding in his tent. I'm starting to wish Joanne really could do telepathy with Fax, not only because that would stop them talking out loud to each other, but also because he'd probably put the tent up for us, under the guise of doing it 'for m'lady'.

We both stand there and have a bit of a cry. Then I feel invigorated and decide to take charge of the situation. I crack open the Pernod and, after slopping some into Daniel, give Joanne the bottle to slug from:

"Let's just take stock of the situation for now."

Joanne has a huge swig of Pernod which makes her go a bit green.

"We haven't got a tent yet."

"Agreed."

"And neither of us knows how to put a tent up."

"Yeah sort of…"

"No sort of about it. If you knew how to put the tent up you'd have put it up, instead of leaving us in a pile of sticks and Pernod. Now. Serious answer – do you know how to put a tent up or not?"

"…No."

"Alright then." Once again I get to do the 'I'm not angry, I'm just disappointed' face. "Well let's work together to get this tent up, and then we'll go find Fax. Agreed?"

I shouldn't have reminded her about Fax.

"But I need to find him NOW or he'll go off with a goddess!"

Is it possible that Joanne's more mental sober than I am pissed? Whatever, I'm past caring.

"We put the tent up and then we go find Fax. No arguing."

"…Fine. God."

An hour later we have something approaching a tent. I am beyond relief. It's tent shaped, that'll do. I think the flap things are missing, but they don't seem to be that important. Unfortunately, when we try to crawl inside, the whole fucking thing collapses. After half an hour of scrabbling round on the floor and some more crying, we realise we haven't got all the corner things that hold the poles together. They were there when we first started doing the tent, and now someone's fucking eaten them or something.

I don't know what these corner things are called but we haven't got all of them. It's no good asking nearby hippies 'have you seen our corner things?', they'd just look at us. So we settle for the next best thing, which is panicking and eating the ends of Joanne's joints that she's found in her bag. I'm not sure eating a joint actually works, but we are calmer.

An unfamiliar voice pipes up. "Do you guys need something to stick it together?" We look round at the voice and Lute Man is offering us a roll of Sellotape. His voice is unfamiliar because he isn't trying to sing 'Greensleeves' in a weird high octave. Turns out he's been watching our never-ending struggle, and it didn't once occur to him to help. I'd like to put his lute up his bum right now. I mutter this to Joanne and she must have heard a bit of it, because she mutters "What?" while grabbing my sleeve.

This doesn't stop me. "Oh fucking thanks you fucking lute man. Play your bad lute while we struggle, and probably starve, and then offer us some God knows what."

"Sellotape" hisses Joanne.

"Fucking whatever." I snatch the Sellotape out of his hand. "And just fucking what are we supposed to do with this? Because I'd like to tape your lute shut is what I'd like to do with it."

He's gone all red. "I just thought, you know, you could tape your tent up or something." He has a snort of something from a bottle.

"Tape? You fucking, fucking penis!"

Joanne nips me in the arm. This does not help my mood. I do a windmill at Lute Man.

"Well you know, stick the corners together or something?"

Joanne pipes up – "How come you've brought Sellotape to a festival? That's, like, brilliant."

Right that's it I'm retiring. I grab the Pernod and park myself in the corner of the bit we've commandeered. Fuck tents. Fuck Sellotape. Fuck everything. I'm not getting up until Joanne has sorted the tent out, even if I go on fire.

Joanne takes the Sellotape from Lute Man, but instead of fixing our tent with it, she uses the Sellotape as an excuse to sit down and start talking about tarot cards, like she hasn't spent enough time today talking about tarot cards. If her tarot cards were that good she would have fucking seen that we'd need those corner things.

I hear Lute Man say "Your friend's a bit angry…"

"Yeah," Joanne replies. "Her chakras are terrible and all out of alignment. She'll be fine once she holds my obsidian."

"And has some more booze, and then beats herself to death with her own luggage," I mutter.

I tune out while Joanne finally gets to work with the tent. Spurred on by the prospect of an actual end to this problem and subsequently finding Fax, she's started doing stuff. I'm impressed. Ten minutes later, the tent doesn't collapse when we get inside it. Now if we can just stay perfectly still for the rest of our lives, maybe it'll be OK. We edge back out without touching the sides.

Joanne throws my things and hers into the tent. "Right it is time to go find Fax."

"Off you go then," I reply, pulling my suitcase back out of the tent. "I'll stay here and guard our stuff."

"What? Don't be silly. God, no one's gonna nick anything off us here. Plus, Chris says he'll keep an eye on our stuff."

"Chris?"

She points towards Lute Man, who at that exact moment is engrossed in trying to extract something he's dropped in his lute. After shaking it so hard he nearly twats himself in the face, he holds up a half-smoked cigarette in triumph. He waves at us, our spat from earlier apparently forgotten.

"That guy? No fucking way. He'll probably smoke our stuff."

"God don't be so dramatic! Look, come with me to find Fax before he meets someone else and goes off with her, and then we can all have chips."

I don't want chips, I want to be left alone. And anyway,

the chips here won't even be real chips made out of potatoes; they'll be weird hippy chips made from seaweed and hemp.

"Sorry, you're not moving me." I settle back down on the floor ready to get a mystery bottle out of my suitcase. "Look, go find Fax, and do whatever it is you do when you people greet each other; I'll be here when you get back." I pull out a bottle of brown looking stuff that I don't remember buying, let alone packing. Oh well.

"Yo is that booze? Can I have some?"

For fuck's sake, Lute Man again. What is it with hippies and wanting to have your stuff?

"Be nice to him," Joanne hisses. "He helped us put the tent up." He did no such thing, but there's something in her face that makes me decide not to argue. And anyway, if I agree to be nice to Lute Man, she'll hopefully piss off for a bit.

"Fine." Since the tent's up and we're not homeless any more, I suppose I should make a bit of an effort to be nice. I call over to Lute Man. "Bring a cup over or whatever."

"Sweet, be right there!" He dives back into his tent, and I swear I hear breaking glass.

Joanne goes then. I'm amazed she's lasted this long. I can't tell what this brown stuff is from drinking it, and the label's all peeled off. Whatever, it hasn't killed me so far.

Part of me is actually quite excited about meeting Fax. I want to know if that tattoo really is Jason Donovan. I try not to think about him teaming up with Lute Man for a special rendition of 'Feet Of Leaves'.

Lute Man lurches over to our bit of area and plops himself down. I slop some of the brown stuff into a plastic glass he produces (no idea what he broke in his tent) and then things are peaceful for a while. He lights up a cigarette and I let him crap on about how he's going to be playing his lute at something called 'Music as the hidden talisman for raising your vibrations'. I hope he gets his string fixed before then.

I'm just settling down into something approaching calm, when I hear a familiar voice a few feet away:

"Oh God Titania, people are *smoking* around here. Don't they care at all about my allergies?"

Oh fucking Christing tits.

It's not her.

It's not.

It fucking is.

22. ENEMIES

Shit. Fucking Titania and her friend. Of all the acres and acres of land (I assume, I blocked most of it out), they deliberately find us so they can come and disapprove next to us. That's the only possible explanation. They are seeking revenge for me nearly killing Titania's friend by drinking near her.

They seem to be parked a few tents over. That means they might have been here before us, but that makes no difference. They still knew I was going to be here, so they deliberately put their tent up near mine so they could spend the weekend claiming I'm trying to kill them.

They're waddling over to their tent, armed with horrible hairy bags. With them is one of the fattest women I've ever seen, including all the Drayton Manor hazards at Slimming World. The fat woman has decided that the most flattering piece of clothing she owns is a rainbow striped jumper, which she has teamed with fairy wings. It's an interesting look.

I don't think they've spotted me, but they've definitely sensed that there's smoking going on, for which I must be entirely responsible. This is confirmed when they get to their tent, put their bags down, then immediately all look over in my direction, as one. I'm trying to figure out if the fat one has her own tent. She must have, she can't possibly fit in a tent with those two.

The sky clouds over and small animals flee the land as the three of them march over to us. Titania's friend glares at Lute Man. Titania coughs pointedly. Rainbow jumper looks hungry.

Lute Man is completely oblivious to their presence, because he's been snorting stuff out of a bottle. He's lying on his back with the plastic glass balanced on his chest, attempting to blow smoke rings.

Titania coughs again, but louder. I start laughing into my drink. I hope Lute Man tells them to fuck right off, but I suspect he'll just offer them some Sellotape.

"Cough cough." No response. She tries me instead.

"Cough cough."

Then she recognises me. Her face shrivels up.

"Oh, I might have known you'd have something to do with this."

Why? Why on earth 'might' she have known that? There are thousands of people here; is it really likely that I'm going to be the only one smoking? And as some sort of plot to annoy her and her friends?

What am I talking about? I'm not even the one doing the fucking smoking.

Titania's friend has her hands over her nose and mouth. The fat one is rubbing her back and offering her a paper bag to breathe into. I could suggest she helps herself by fucking off, but that might not do any good.

I shrug. "I'm not smoking, he is."

She turns back to her friend. "It's OK Felicity, she's going to stop smoking now."

What the hell is wrong with these people? "I'm not fucking smoking! And even if I was, I wouldn't stop just because she's decided to come stand next to me and have a fake illness, *again*."

I carry on before Titania can reply. "I didn't even want to come to this fucking place, I'm doing it as a favour to my friend. Not only have I already had to put up with coming here on the fucking B.O. Bus, which you somehow managed to make *even more unbearable* by demanding I stayed conscious throughout, now you expect me to put up with your nonsense again? What's next? What else is she going to decide she's allergic to? Air?

She starts to reply again, but I'm not going to let her reply until I'm finished – "And, AND – I'M NOT EVEN FUCKING SMOKING! HE IS!"

Her face has turned into a bumhole through sheer indignation. "Look, there's no need to be so defensive. Cigarette smoke makes Felicity go light headed, therefore you shouldn't be smoking round here."

She hasn't directed any of this at Lute Man, just at me. It becomes very important that I defend Lute Man's right to smoke.

"Look you fucking vegan, this is the bottom line. You cannot order strangers to stop doing something just because you don't personally like doing that thing. Did you grow up so spoilt that you honestly don't know that? You know what? I hope everyone in this fucking place smokes except for you two. And as for her –"

I point at 'Felicity', but Titania butts in.

"How dare you! I'm going to report you for air pollution and invasion of a safe space!"

That's it. That's fucking it. I grab Lute Man's pack of cigarettes from next to him. Must remember to check he's not dead in a minute. I wave the packet at Titania

"I don't even fucking smoke. But guess what, I'm going to start smoking, right now, just to piss you off!"

I put all Lute Man's remaining cigarettes in my mouth at once and light them. I smoked for about a year when I was a teenager, but I was never much good at it. So getting back into the habit by smoking ten cigarettes at once is a bit difficult, but this is a matter of honour.

I blow as much smoke as I can at them, while jumping up and down. The effort is making me cough a bit. Hopefully any onlookers will just think this is performance art.

The fat one chimes in – "Just wait until my best friend gets back! He knows karate!"

This distracts Titania. "Don't worry Bee, leave it to me. I don't want you to get into a potentially triggering situation." She turns back to me. "You are a disgusting person with no respect for your fellow beings!"

"MELISSA! WHAT THE FUCK ARE YOU DOING!"

I stop jumping up and down. Joanne's back, and she looks cross. I can't answer Joanne because my mouth is still full of cigarettes. It doesn't occur to me to take them out.

The fat one squeals and looks past Joanne. "Fax! Fax, this woman is trying to burn Titania with cigarettes!"

Right, two things:

1. Is that fat one a bit simple.
2. Oh my God, in person Fax *really* looks like Laurence Llewellyn-Bowen.

23. M'LADY

The three vegans from hell crowd around Fax, trying to get me into trouble. Joanne gets my side of the story. Wires are uncrossed, pieces are put together, and we discover that the 'group of friends' Fax was going to the festival with have turned out to be the Witches of Eastwick. Titania is slightly mollified by this turn of events, given that she can now bitch to Joanne about "your horrible tent mate who tried to verbally assault me and then lunged at me with some lit cigarettes", as well as continuing their dull-as-fuck bus conversation about tarot cards.

Joanne tells me off, more for show than anything else. For all she pisses me off, I know she's not mental enough to believe I actually tried to burn Titania with a cigarette. I'll be honest though, I only didn't do that because I didn't think of it. They seem to be behaving better towards me now that Joanne and Fax are here, anyway.

Lute Man chooses this moment to wonder where his cigarettes have gone. Luckily the others don't hear him. I panic and tell him a dog came along and ate them. He seems to accept this – "That's cool, I nicked those ones off someone anyway." He goes back to his tent to "score" another packet; he doesn't come back out and then I can hear snoring.

What with all the drama, I haven't been introduced to Fax yet. Joanne pulls him over to me, then stands there doing a 'ta-da' motion. This is Joanne's version of a formal introduction.

Fax kisses my hand and says "A ha, splendid to meet thou." It takes all the muscles in my face to stop myself laughing. I suspect that 'must not laugh' is going to become the default setting for the next few days.

Fax does precisely nothing to help matters with his next line: "So you're m'lady's handmaiden?"

What? What am I? I need to get some of that face freezing stuff if I'm going to survive the next few days.

"Er, yes…?" I hope he's not expecting me to join in with the medieval bollocks. I fall back on my natural ice breaker. "Would you like a drink?"

I just know, in my heart of hearts, that he's going to ask if I've got any mead. If he does that my face dam is going to burst and all the laughing is going to come out. So I hurry off to my suitcase before he can say that. I know this is important to Joanne, so I pull all the bottles out of my suitcase and line them up. I'm not sure if I should offer my three enemies a drink. Titania's friend will accuse me of trying to poison her with fumes.

It doesn't matter anyway because when I look round they've fucked off back to their tent. I can just see Rainbow Jumper's arse poking out of a flap.

"We have Pernod, ouzo, and this brown stuff which is quite nice."

Fax turns to Joanne. "Your friend is quite the bar wench." I stuff my fist in my mouth.

Joanne grabs Fax's voluminous sleeve. "Come and see our tent! I put it up all by myself!" I don't say anything, I'm too busy trying to find something to put Fax's drink in. I didn't plan for this, I've only brought Daniel. I guess I can make the sacrifice.

As I'm slopping some ouzo into Daniel, a bad thought occurs to me. I wasn't supposed to be drinking out of Daniel, because Daniel has had piss and bleach in him. And now I've been drinking out of him and I might die. No, I'll definitely die. But worse than I will definitely die is I have to give a pissed-in cup to Fax, because it's the only one I've got. Do I risk killing Joanne's boyfriend so I don't look rude?

Joanne solves the problem for me by taking Daniel from my hand. She shows no sign of remembering why drinking out of Daniel is a bad thing, so I don't push the issue.

"Who's this fellow on your mug?" asks Fax.

Joanne answers before I can. "Oh, that's a guy she used to go out with I think."

What? Is that what she's thought all this time? That I used to go out with Daniel O'Donnell?

"Jo you do know who that is really don't you?"

"Yeah, it's Daniel your ex-boyfriend."

"Why do you think I used to go out with Daniel O'Donnell?"

She just looks at me. Fax watches the conversation like it's a tennis match.

"What?"

"You know Daniel O'Donnell is a famous singer right?"

"Oh is he? Is that why you stopped going out with him?"

I have a swig of the Pernod. "No, I've never been out with him. I've never even met him, he's just famous. My mum likes him, we've had that cup since I was little."

She thinks this over, and after a minute seems to understand. "Oh right! That makes sense I guess. I just assumed he was a guy you broke up with and you missed him so you had his photo put on a mug."

God, if you just let me be drunk for the rest of my life, I promise I'll never ask for anything again.

Joanne turns to Fax. "I'd have your photo put on a mug."

Then they look at each other for a bit.

"Melissa's sorry about that thing with your friends, aren't you Mel?"

"Yes I am." I'm no such fucking thing.

Fax waves it away. "That's OK, Felicity has sensitive nerves. I did tell her that an open air festival might be too much for her but she was determined to come. She wants to see the live performance of *L'Enfoiré Bleu* in the radical arts tent."

"I heard they were doing *The Nude Iliad* in that tent," says Joanne.

"Yes, my tarot reader is playing the part of Agamemnon. She's incredibly talented."

I top up Fax's drink, and steer the conversation away from nude plays. "So Fax, what do you do?"

He smiles. "I write poetry, and I try to be one with the essences at all times."

I was expecting something like 'I'm a welder'. I should have fucking known.

"Right. Great." No fucking clue what to say now. "Does it pay well?" I feel like someone's dad trying to make conversation at a birthday party. I'll be asking him what he thinks of the new Ford Cortina next.

"God Mel, money isn't the only thing in the world," snaps Joanne. "Fax isn't, like, a commercial poet, not like those sell-outs."

"Oh, OK… sorry?"

"What you really meant was 'How does he get money?'

I mean, like it matters. You people are so obsessed with money." She starts to tell Fax about the time I made her pay for a Creme Egg, but I cut her off.

"To be fair, that is what most people mean when they say 'what do you do'."

For all Joanne's indignation, Fax doesn't seem offended. "I *do* toil in exchange for modern currency, but my essential self is in my poetry."

"Oh right OK." I know he wants me to ask him about his poetry. I know the minute I seem even vaguely interested he'll start reciting it. I'm trying to put that off for as long as possible. I bet it doesn't even rhyme. "I just work at the Co-op, so..."

Joanne chimes in again. "Fax's poetry is brilliant. He writes about your soul."

"What, mine specifically?"

She gives me a look. "No, your soul in general. And castles."

I'm starting to get confused with all the souls and castles and toil. It's the Pernod. Maybe I should leave them to it? I could go have a lie down in our crap tent. I'm not sure I want to leave Daniel in the care of Fax and Joanne though, they might involve him in some kind of weird sex ritual.

A woman in what looks like a grass skirt dances past. She's carrying a ribbon on a stick. Joanne and Fax don't react; they're busy talking about some soul searching bullshit. I catch the words 'erotic spoon'. Right, tent time. I do a big theatrical yawn. "You know what guys, I might have a very quick nap, just so I'm full of beans for later." I don't mention that I'm going to try to make a quick nap last four days.

24. SOCIALISING

It's getting dark when I wake up. I poke my head out of the tent but Joanne and Fax are nowhere to be seen. I wonder if they've gone to see the sex play.

God I could murder a coffee. I wonder if Joanne's brought a camping stove? Not that I'd know how to use it.

"Yo."

I look round. Lute Man is sitting outside his tent.

"Oh, hello."

"Your friends have gone over there."

He points towards Titania's tent. Fuck.

I take stock of my surroundings. Sadly I'm still at this bloody festival. And I realise that I really need a piss. I hope they have toilets here, not just some horrible vegan excuses for toilets, where you have to wipe yourself with leaves.

The need for a wee prompts me to start manoeuvring my body in order to extract it from the tent. This is easier said than done. When I find myself with one foot wedged into the pointy bit of the tent, I start to consider just doing a piss in the tent. However, I'd probably regret this later. I push on, and by adopting a strategy of alternately pulling muscles and calling the tent a bastard, I manage to get free.

Lute Man is still sitting there. Once again he has watched my struggle and made no attempt to help.

"Yo, you want some poppers?"

What? I guess this is him trying to help.

"Not today thank you. Look can you watch my tent and stuff? I'm off to find the loo."

"Sure thing." He picks up his lute and starts trying to play what sounds terrifyingly like a Spice Girls song. I head out into the darkness, trying to look casual as I attempt to hold the wee in my fanny.

As I wander around searching for something resembling a cubicle, I start to realise I should have paid more attention to where we parked our tent. Oh well, no time for that now. The universe is smiling on me because I find a row of Portaloos. Once that business is taken care of, I realise even more that I really should have paid attention to where the tent was. Maybe I should have tied some string to it. Or brought any string to do that with in the first place.

All I can see now are identical tents dotted around, a few campfires, and a stall selling burgers. Oh God, burgers. I'm really very hungry indeed. I should have packed something other than Freddos. Maybe I'll go get some money, then come back here and... no, I can't be fucked with that. They're probably burgers made of grass or something anyway.

Right, time to find the tent again. I listen very carefully in case I can hear lute music, but the selfish bastard has stopped. Either that or I'm a mile away from the tent, I can't tell.

OK. Shit. I'm starting to panic a bit now. I might be faced with the task of checking every tent here to see if it's mine or not.

Five minutes later I am stumbling round in a nightmare. There are about 37,000 tents, and they all look and smell exactly the same.

"Whoops"

"Sorry, excuse me"

"Oh, that's a nice dream catcher you've got there"

"Sorry"

"Evening"

This goes on for fucking ever. All the hippies look at me with vague interest but aren't bothered enough to actually wonder who I am or what I'm doing.

Just when I'm starting to think I'm going to have to sleep on the floor and start again in the morning, I hear a horribly familiar sound:

"HAHA FAX THAT IS SO FUNNEEE!"

This is followed by a death rattle kind of laugh. It's fucking Titania, cackling like a pile of old corpses. Under normal circumstances, I think I would have curled into a ball and quietly rolled away upon hearing this, but I don't care for now, I'm just relieved to be back near my own tent.

I make my way towards the noise, and eventually collapse outside my tent. Lute Man is still sitting there; for reasons known only to him, he is now wearing sunglasses.

"Yo, I watched your stuff for you."

"What? Yes, yes good job."

Joanne appears out of the darkness. "Where have you been? We're all sitting round the fire. Fax is telling us about that time the SAS begged him to join but he couldn't because he was busy that day." She gestures to Lute Man. "Chris are you coming to hang out with us?"

Chris. Must remember that. Must stop calling him Lute Man.

Wait, is Joanne now expecting me to go sit round a fire with my three mortal enemies? I'd hate to give Titania's friend diabetes just by looking at her.

"I'm not sure Fax's friends like me very much Jo. You two go though, I'll just hang round here and get sorted out." There's nothing like drinking neat ouzo from the bottle while trying to block out your surroundings for getting sorted out.

"Oh they were just being silly. It was, like, a misunderstanding. Come on, we've got food."

Shit, food. I like food. I remember that I was going to try and get back to that burger stall, but if I'm honest I was lucky to find my way back here once. Oh well, I might as well go to their tent and get it over with, otherwise the next four days is going to be spent pretending to be dead when I see Titania approaching. Plus I can eat their food.

"Bring all your booze."

All of it? Unless Joanne means for me to sit there and drink all my remaining booze myself, I resent this plan. Oh fuck it, I can always get some more tomorrow. I decide to make the effort for Joanne, and for Fax who, despite being odd and full of shit, seems quite nice.

We gather up the half empty bottles and make our way over to their tent. Chris follows us, carrying his lute. If he tries to play 'Greensleeves' again I might have to accidentally chop the lute up for firewood and put it on the fire.

When we get there, the first thing I see is Titania's friend, who is sitting smoking a bong. She is smoking a fucking bong. After all that shit she put me through earlier. I assume smoke only makes her ill when it means someone else is having a good time then. That's it, I'm going to shove that bong up her arse.

Joanne notes my growing rage, and my death glare pointed at Titania's friend. She grabs my sleeve and whispers "Yeah I know, I think she just lies about stuff for attention. An hour ago she told me that breathing unfiltered air gave her lead poisoning. I don't believe that. I think she might be a bit weird."

Well at least I'm not on my own with this any more. Now I know Joanne's on my side, it might be easier to spend time with these women without burning the festival down. I'll make an effort.

"Guys, you've met Melissa, and this is Chris, our neighbour. Chris, this is Fax, and Titania, and Felicity, and Bee."

I think the stupid lying one is Felicity, and the fat one is Bee. She is still wearing the fairy wings. Titania gives me a look but doesn't say anything.

Fax is in the middle of some story or other. I assume it's his made up SAS one, because I catch the line "I taught Ross Kemp how to get rid of a wasps nest."

Joanne doesn't miss a beat. She heads straight back to Fax and rewards his fibbing with staring at him and stroking his ridiculous big sleeve.

I'm not offered any bong. Fuck them, I didn't want any anyway. As punishment, they're not getting any of my brown stuff. I wish I knew what it was. At least no one appears to be drinking out of Daniel; he must be back at the tent. That would have been a step too far.

Fax approaches the fire and I start panicking a bit. He's definitely going to get his sleeves caught in the fire, and I don't think there's a hospital here. I don't think you can treat burns with lavender soap. He pulls a tray out of the bottom of the fire while my bum muscles clench up into my neck. Phew, no human fireball. He offers the tray round and we all take a… thing of… food? I think?

It's hard to see in the dark, but it looks like some kind of meatball. Meatballs should not be green. Joanne sees me inspecting mine.

"It's a kale and facon savoury orb."

"It's a fucking what?"

She tuts. "They're yummy."

I don't see her eating hers. "I think we should have come a bit more prepared you know. I'll probably go stock up on burgers and stuff in the morning."

She looks at me like I've just offered to shit in the campfire. "God, there's, like, no meat allowed here! Seriously Mel, just go with it."

"What, there's no meat allowed at the entire festival?"

"No, it's a safe space."

"Who for, fucking cows?"

She ignores me then. I take the tiniest possible bite of my 'savoury orb'. It tastes of chronic depression. But fuck it, I'm hungry. And I guess it is free food. I hope those cows are fucking grateful.

25. CLASS WAR

An hour later we're all pleasantly pissed again. I've been observing the fat one called Bee. She doesn't say much; she mostly alternates between gazing longingly at Fax and glaring at Joanne. A-ha. This could develop into some interesting drama. Part of me hopes there's a fight at some point. Not that I really want Joanne to get injured or anything, but I'm bored.

I don't understand people who claim they don't enjoy watching fights. It's such a lie – everyone loves standing round watching fights and drama. There's a pub up the road from our house, and sometimes we'll go hang out there at closing time in case the regulars start hitting each other. It's cheaper than getting a real hobby. Sometimes that weird man with the Lidl carrier bag will stand on our street shouting at himself, but that's not really the same.

Anyway, it's becoming increasingly clear that Bee is friendzoned by Fax. I wonder how many other female admirers Fax has. The mind boggles.

Everyone's having their own little conversations, but somehow Titania and Felicity's conversation manages to rise above the others:

"It's so nice to be amongst people like myself. Where

I live, there are lots of *working class people*, so good luck trying to engage them in conversation ha ha!"

I keep listening as Titania and Felicity start listing their imagined crimes of the 'working class people' in Titania's town. These include:

- Having jobs where you actually have to do stuff
- Wearing football shirts
- Wishing her 'Merry Christmas' (*"It's so culturally insensitive"*)
- Having mobile phones and looking at them

"My neighbour is called 'Bob'. Can you imagine!" Fresh snorts of laughter from the pair of them. "Do you know, once he told me he was thinking of going to *Benidorm* for his holiday! I mean, he's nice enough in his own little way, but – how shall I put this – you wouldn't invite him to a book club supper..."

I like the sound of Bob. I hope that when Titania gets back to her house all her furniture has been stolen, and that Bob is stood there pointing and laughing. I wish I was in Benidorm with Bob.

Felicity chimes in: "Yes well you know that unfortunately my road is near a block of flats, and I don't want to begin to imagine what goes on in them."

Titania crows sympathetically.

"I mean, as you know I'm extremely broad minded. I don't look down on people simply because of their class. I do vote Labour, after all. And I do know a working class lady. I believe her name is Pam, or Pat. Oh it doesn't matter. She works in the shop where I buy my *Guardian*..."

They crap on like this for another ten minutes, as I start to wonder if I'm dreaming this whole conversation. I can't tell if they hate what they call 'working class people', or if they like having them around, like pets.

"I mean, good for her that she has a little job in a shop,

but sometimes I think she... oh, it's terribly *un-pc* to say this... but sometimes I think these people *forget their place.*"

"Mm hmm" crows Titania, her mouth full of kale and facon.

"Now, I'm not saying that the working class people don't deserve the same respect as you or I. After all, we are a tolerant country. But there is a natural *order* to things, and the poorly-educated must realise that educated people are paid more for a reason."

"I so agree" says Titania. "It's important to have people who serve in shops, and people to empty bins. These people do vitally important work. But they mustn't forget that this is not necessarily *skilled* work, not like homeopathy consultation."

That's fucking it. "I work in a shop" I say, louder than I mean to. Then I stare at them.

"I beg your pardon?" says Felicity.

"I work in a shop."

The backtracking begins once they realise I've been listening to their entire conversation. It's apparently one thing to slag off the working class when you're among friends, but it's a massive faux pas to actually insult one to its face.

Titania and Felicity plaster grins to their faces. "Oh well done, oh good for you! We were just talking about how shop assistants are so *down to earth*, and so... so *real.*"

I'm about to go over there and kick them in their smug faces, but Fax stands up and announces that it's "music time". It's probably the wrong thing to do to start a fist fight in the middle of Fax's music time, so I don't. Instead I file this in my non-imaginary list of 'shit Titania has done for which she must be punished'.

On hearing the words 'music time', Chris takes his

sunglasses off and picks up his lute. Fax says "Hey man, a duet! Do you know 'I Gave My Love A Cherry?' It's nice on the lute."

This is a bizarre situation. For all intents and purposes, Fax is the alpha male here, but I don't think alpha males are supposed to get all excited about singing 'I Gave My Love A Cherry'. Andrew Lincoln wouldn't sit around singing 'I Gave My Love A Cherry'. Whatever, the other women seem to love him. Joanne has started applauding before they've even done anything.

They launch into what I think is supposed to be 'I Gave My Love A Cherry', except sadly they seem to be playing it in two different keys. It hurts my ears. Joanne has stood up and is doing some weird circular dancing. Bee is still staring at Fax.

When it finally stops we all launch into rapturous applause. Titania goes and gets a tambourine out of her tent, which I'm sure is going to make the situation ten times better. Fax and Chris move onto murdering 'Scarborough Fair'. Fax gets overexcited and starts shouting whenever he sings the word 'parsley', which makes me have to stuff my fist in my mouth again.

Then they do a song that I don't know the name of, but which involves them stamping their feet a lot. I'm sure the chorus includes the word 'nipple'. I'm starting to get very tired now. Maybe I should head off to bed, as fucking unmissable as this is. I stand up.

"Right, proper bedtime for me I think. Don't want to be tired for tomorrow."

I leave them and pick my way over to our tent. I should get a decent night's sleep; no doubt Joanne's going to be staying in Fax's tent tonight. When I get back I need a wee again, There's no fucking way I'm making that 20 mile round trip again, so I just do a wee next to the tent.

It's OK, I don't think anyone's seen me. Then I dive into the tent and land face first. I don't plan to move from this position for at least ten hours.

26. ESSENCES

I am woken up by a shuffling noise. This is bad because there isn't anything in the tent that should be shuffling. I am far too pissed to care about where it might be coming from though, so I doze back off.

I'm woken up again, and this time I realise there's someone in the tent. I mean, apart from me. I'm about to panic when I remember that Joanne's using this tent as well. I vaguely wonder why she isn't spending the night with Fax, but this is cut short by my falling asleep again.

I wake up for a third time, and am just about to shout at Joanne for waking me up, when I hear Fax say "I would pull the stars out of the sky for you."

My first thought is 'I'm sure he's nicked that from a song'. My second thought is 'Oh fucking hell no, don't tell me they're both in this fucking tent with me.' I shut my eyes again and will myself to go back to sleep, assuming Joanne and Fax are about to do the same.

They don't go to sleep. There is more shuffling, and after the shuffling has gone on for a few minutes, the worst thought in the world occurs to me. No. They wouldn't dare. They're not going to do that, Please God they're not going to do that.

Joanne starts giggling. I quickly try to think of a way to kill myself before they can get any further. It doesn't occur to me to confront them: that would mean I'd have to acknowledge that I've heard them up until this point. Oh God, I don't know what to do.

I put my hands over my ears, but I can still bloody hear them.

"I am a she-Goddess!"

"Hang on, my leg's bent wrong."

"Oh Fax you mountain lion!"

"...Your essences..."

At one point Fax starts singing 'I Gave My Love A Cherry' again. This is the worst thing that has ever happened to anyone, ever. Maybe if I count to a billion I can block them out. I get as far as seven before they start up again with "This angle gets my chi going..."

My hands are now pressed so hard against my ears that I think my ears might be bleeding. A foot kicks me. I start with my counting again, and this time I get as far as thirty seven, and then it starts to sound like there are farm animals in the tent. I swear one of them moos. I start counting again.

Three hundred and forty eight, three hundred and forty nine...

I never, ever want to hear about or talk about or do sex ever again. I don't even want to see the word 'sextuple' written in a book about maths. Not that I'm likely to ever read a book about maths.

I think they're finally asleep. I wonder how I'm going to face the pair of them in the morning. I go back to sleep and have a weird dream about that woman off the *Daily Politics* chasing me with a pen.

27. CHICORY

I wake up and am immediately traumatised by the events of last night. This must be how it feels if you've been in a war.

Joanne and Fax are gone, which gets rid of my main problem for a bit. I think the thing to do is just try to pretend it never happened, and to never look Joanne or Fax in the eye ever again.

I should probably get sorted out now I've survived the night. I need a wash and a change of clothes, and some food that once had a pulse. I have no idea where the showers are here, or even if they have any. Maybe you're just expected to rub yourself down with herbs, I don't know. Whatever, I'm not going off on a trek like yesterday. I don't have to anyway – I've brought some baby wipes, they're in my suitcase next to my spatula weapon.

I give myself a going over and pull on some clean clothes. Moving around in the tent seems a bit easier today, I must be getting the hang of it.

Joanne and Fax aren't hanging round outside, thank God. Chris is sitting outside his tent again.

"Morning."

"Yo, are you gonna come and watch me in my thing

tonight?"

Oh yeah, he's got a lute performance. I hope he's tuned the bloody thing by then. He's caught me off guard because I say "Yes, that will be lovely." I stop to yawn. "Have you got any coffee?"

"No. I've got some bennies if you want one?"

I don't know what those are, and I don't want to know.

"They're sort of for emergencies though. They make you proper shit yourself."

"I'll pass thanks."

I decide I'm going to have to go on an expedition if today is going to be bearable.

"Do you know where they sell coffee?"

He has a think. "Well the main bit is that way, so..."

He points in what I think is the direction of the toilets. I'm going to have to risk it if I want coffee. I should be OK if I pay attention. Plus it's not dark any more.

"Right, cheerio."

Finding the 'main bit' isn't nearly as hard as it was last night, but now there are a lot more people milling around. I find the burger stall again; it's a good job I didn't come back here for a burger, because they're not real burgers. I should have fucking known. Jesus – 'gluten-free superfood burgers'. I'll bet my fucking house that there's nothing super about them.

There is, inexplicably, a maypole next to the burger stall. Not sure how I missed that last night. It seems to be the meeting place for people. I make a mental note to remember it in case I ever want to have any contact with Joanne ever again.

I walk a bit further and – thank fucking Christ – find a place selling coffee. I'm a bit tempted to buy a bucket and just ask them to fill it up. After discarding this as a shit idea, I order a double espresso. The girl behind the counter looks at me.

"Oh, sorry, we don't do expresso."

I assume they don't do the thing I asked for either. "But you do do coffee right?"

"Well, yes, we do chicory drink."

"Chicory... right. Is there caffeine in that?"

"Oh, no, don't worry, everything is 100% natural."

Oh fucking hell. I just want a coffee. Don't make me go back and take one of Chris' scary sounding 'bennies'. "Don't you do any proper coffee?"

"Well, we sell chicory drink, which is an excellent natural alternative to coffee."

"Fine whatever, give me a huge cup of that please."

She hands over what would be a 'medium' in Costa. "Eight pounds please."

I have precisely £3.50 with me, because there is no way on Earth that a cup of coffee is going to cost more than £3.50. I must have misheard her.

"Sorry, that sounded like you said eight."

"Yes, eight pounds please."

"For a paper cup of fake coffee."

"It's natural chicory drink."

"Whatever. What it's not is worth eight quid."

I don't think the girl knows quite what to do. I don't think she's ever been challenged like this before. Before she can ask me for the drink back, I take a gulp. It's fucking disgusting. Definitely not worth eight quid.

The girl is looking round frantically. I think she's hoping some policemen are going to magically show up and arrest me for not paying for shit fake coffee. I decide to make her a deal.

"Look, I have £3.50 on me. I wasn't expecting to have to pay eight quid for a drink, because frankly that's a ridiculous price. I'm happy to give you all the money I have though."

She'll have to accept this because it's not like she can demand the drink back and then give it to someone else. "I can wait here for you to go get some more money then."

"No, I won't be doing that. I'll be giving you £3.50 or nothing, because this is a cup of hot mud."

Then I notice something that immediately wins me the argument. "There are no prices written anywhere. That is against the law." I'm fucked if I know whether that's true or not, but I bet it is. If it isn't illegal it should be. I bet she just charges what she feels like after she's made the drink.

Right. I channel some Co-op officialese:

"I think you'll find that, according to paragraph 27, clause 8 of the FSA's 'service of beverages and sundries' guidelines, all prices must be clearly displayed to the customer before any transaction takes place."

I really should have trained as a lawyer. I've seen *Columbo*. Actually, was Columbo a lawyer? Maybe he was a rozzer instead.

The girl has no fucking clue what I'm talking about or if I'm right. So she just says "OK, I'll take the £3.50. But no one else has argued against my prices."

I dare say her normal customers are people who think paying eight quid for something is a badge of honour. I must tell Titania and Felicity about this place. I hand over the money, more to keep the peace than anything else. I'd hate her to actually look into my rules and see they're made up.

I feel much better as I wander back to the tent. The 'chicory drink' is horrible, but I'm going to drink it out of principle.

28. SPOONS

Joanne and Fax are there when I get back. Fax has his sodding guitar out again. Interestingly, he's also got a tie round his head like Rambo. It's probably not a tie. There's probably some fancy technical name for it. He still looks a dick.

All I can think as I approach them is 'I heard you having sex, I heard you having sex, I heard you having sex…' Oh God. Right, I'll be OK as long as I keep the conversation on trivial subjects like the weather and not the fact that Fax is a mountain lion.

Joanne sees me first. "Hiiiiii! Oh wow you got coffee, where did you get coffee?"

"It's not coffee, it's hot mud," I explain.

Joanne carries on. "This morning we're going to do a spoon carving, and later we're going to watch Chris' lute performance. He's doing a Celtic folk medley."

"It's intended to be listened to while holding chakra crystals," says Fax. "Did you bring yours?"

"Oh shit I forgot them," I reply. "Are you two on your own today?"

Translation: 'Am I going to have to breathe the same air as those three bearded witches for one second'.

Joanne answers while fiddling with a Rizla. "Felicity and Tit have gone to a misogyny awareness picnic. I think Bee has gone to a fairy visualisation and pumice workshop."

What the fuck are these things. Next they're going to tell me about *Find Your Inner Muslim With Embroidery*. I wonder how much of this stuff I'm going to be expected to do. Hopefully 'none' is the answer. "What are you guys doing about breakfast?"

"Well, Fax and I thought we'd have superfood smoothies on the way to the spoon carving. You're coming with us right?"

I sit down without answering. If I say no they'll think I'm being difficult on purpose. If I say yes I'll have to go do spoon carving.

I get a handful of Freddos from my stash and eat them in the tent. When I get back out, Joanne hands me a leaflet featuring a clipart of some leaves, and a list of today's 'events'.

Highlights of the list:

... a seven piece explosion fusing ukulele and Casio keyboard functions

Donna X. Lowry – Vowel Free Poetry

Be at One With Your Microbiology (includes free dirt)

40 minutes of rhythmic poetry dealing with the issue of racism in DIY wholesalers

I'm dismayed to see there's nothing listed under 'sit there and drink yourself into a mild stupor'. I guess I'll go to the spoon carving.

I'm surprised they've invited me actually. I guess I

should be glad she's making the effort, rather than leaving me to be a Billy No Mates while she goes off and has sex with Fax for four days.

Oh, fucking thanks brain. I told you not to mention that. Oh yeah, you can apologise now but the damage is done isn't it? It's a bit fucking late for sorry. Right that's it, I'm going to go carve a spoon just so I've got something to gouge you out of my head with. Happy now?

"OK I'll come and do a spoon. And I don't need, I dunno, a spoon qualification to do it?"

They laugh. "Not at all," says Fax. "The important thing is to visualise the spoon, and to pour your energy into it. Really feel the spoon as you create it."

"And then what, at the end you get a spoon?"

"Yes."

"Wow."

I might as well try to be optimistic. You never know – I might end up becoming obsessed with spoon carving. Maybe I'll discover a whole new career.

When we get to the spoon place I instinctively know that I'm not going to discover a whole new career. The sign says 'Elliot Windsome, master spoon artist'. A woman with muscly arms is sitting next to the sign, doing something with a chisel. Presumably this is Elliot Windsome. I bet she's got loads of spoons at home. I bet she has at least 20 spoons. Maybe she gives them all names.

Her biceps are intimidating She looks like she'd be able to crush my head with her arms if I disapprove of her spoons. Also, there's an axe stuck in the ground next to her.

Joanne approaches her – "Are we in time for the 11 o'clock workshop?"

"Yes, you're early." That's strange – Elliot Windsome has the voice of a nice old lady and the biceps of a large frightening man. "Make yourselves comfortable, we're getting started in about ten minutes."

We sit round in a circle as directed by Elliot Windsome. Why has she got an axe? The rational half of my brain is claiming it's probably for the spoon stuff. The other half is saying it's no such thing – she uses it to murder people if she doesn't like the spoon they make.

I whisper to Joanne. "What's that axe for? What's she going to do with it?"

"What? What are you on about? She cuts your wood out for you with it."

"Really?"

"Yes I think so."

Some more people join us then. Joanne turns back to Fax and they start discussing which type of wood has the best 'aura'. I keep one eye on the axe. Not that I really believe Elliot Windsome is going to just throw the axe at my head for no reason, but you never know with these people.

To my relief she doesn't throw the axe at anyone's head; she doesn't even get it out of the ground. Instead she just hands round bits of wood that she hacked to death earlier. Apparently these are the beginnings of our spoons. Fax gets all excited and cries "Oh fantastic I've got elder wood!" which makes me put my fist in my mouth again.

Elliot Windsome joins us in the circle, and starts to demonstrate getting a spoon shape using a chisel. I've never used a chisel in my life. I think we might have done chisels once at school, but I don't think I got a go on one.

"The important thing is to intuitively go with the grain of the wood."

"Mm-hmm" say the others, like this is obvious to them.

"Keep your chisel strokes small and neat, but don't get too caught up in that. This is your spoon, and the most important thing is that it's hewn individually."

Right, got that. Bash the fuck out of my wood with a chisel. Do it neatly.

Then the mad bitch lets us loose with chisels while she goes off and does something. To my amazement, Joanne is really good at it. She must have done it before. Fax is stroking his bit of wood a bit too much, and talking to it, rather than getting any work done. If we were in a CDT lesson at my school Mr Harrison would have thrown him out now for being weird.

I don't get on so well. After five minutes I have to put my hand up:

"Miss, I've got my chisel stuck in my thing."

She comes over and pulls my stuck chisel out with her big muscles. Ten minutes after this, it's not going very well again. I put my hand up:

"Miss, my thing's gone a bit wrong, can I have another one?"

"Joanne hisses at me – "Stop calling her 'Miss' you weirdo."

Elliot Windsome and her arm guns come over to me again. She inspects my bit of wood. I've accidentally removed most of the part that was going to be the spoon bit. It's just a stick now. She looks at it disapprovingly:

"Oh dear, is this your first time carving a spoon?"

"Yeah, my friend said I just needed to imagine it."

She glances at Joanne and Fax, who thankfully didn't hear me blame them. "Well there is a bit more to it than that dear." She shouldn't be calling me 'dear' when she's got guns like that. "Tell you what, since this is your first time we'll just concentrate on the fine tuning." She fetches another bit of wood that's already spoon shaped. She could have just given me that to start with and saved everyone all this trouble.

I get on OK with using the small knife thing to gouge out the spoon bit, which makes me feel smug. I don't think I've done too badly for a beginner. Then we have to sit around sanding our spoons. This is the easy part, and everyone in the circle starts chatting as they work.

"*You can infuse your spoon with energy, and then use it to stir herbs...*"

"*This hair colour is 100% vegan...*"

"*Legs round her head, and the poetry was extremely thought provoking...*"

"*I'd actually class the Liberal Democrats as a far right group...*"

Then it's time to varnish our spoons. I might be imagining it, but I feel like Elliot Windsome is hovering around me, like she's worried I'm going to drink the varnish. I don't, so there. But I do end up with something approaching a functioning spoon. I'm rather proud of this – after all, I did all the hard parts, like visualising it.

We all have to pay £10 for our spoons. If we don't pay, I assume she confiscates the spoons. I don't want her to confiscate mine, so I dig around in my bag for my purse. But then Fax pipes up:

"Hey, my treat – m'ladies shall have spoons."

That's very nice of him. I let him pay; I consider it compensation for what I had to put up with last night.

Oh for fuck's sake brain, I warned you not to mention that again. Don't piss me off, I've got a spoon now, and I will use it.

29. PRINGLES

A serious problem is developing – we're running out of booze. A scout out of the main shopping bit informs me that you can only buy cider at this festival. Vegans love cider because it's made from apples. I'm not sure if they think vodka is made from beef or something. There's probably some stall somewhere that will sell you a bottle of 'handmade liqueur' for 20 quid, but that's very much a last resort.

There's nothing else for it – I'm going to have to go find a shop. The minute I announce my intention, everyone immediately starts issuing me with shopping lists. Before I know it I've been ordered to fetch cigarettes, Maltesers, and a copy of the *Guardian*. No fucker offers to come with me.

I ask one of the men at the front gate where the nearest shop is. He's wearing a hi-vis vest which means he knows everything. He says he thinks there's a shop about half a mile away. He doesn't ask me to fetch him anything, thank God.

The walk is OK – trees and stuff. There's nothing much around but it feels like I'm back in civilization for a bit. It's only been a day, but when I reach the village I find myself gazing in wonder at the real buildings made of real bricks. I bet the people here drink coffee instead of hot mud. I'm tempted to knock on people's doors and ask them if they've got any spare coffee and electricity, and if I can please live in their house for the next three days.

The woman in the shop gives me a look. I suppose I must look like one of the festival people to her. I've borrowed Joanne's rucksack, which isn't ideal because it's got badges sewn onto it and there are crystals hanging off it. But it will carry a lot of booze, which is the main point.

Right – shopping. Loads of bottles, assorted food that won't break or be interfered with by vegans, jar of coffee (which I will eat raw with my new spoon if I have to). Felicity wants a *Guardian*. Well she's not getting a fucking *Guardian*, because I don't fucking like her. She can have a *Daily Star* instead. I'll just tell her I can't read because I'm working class. Maltesers, more Freddos, ciggies, and some stickers, because they're shiny and I don't get stickers at Slimming World even though I'm supposed to.

The walk back takes ages because I have to keep stopping and checking the bottles are withstanding being bashed together in the rucksack. When I get back to our tent everyone's sprawled out in front of it, apart from Chris who is out somewhere. Fax is flanked by Joanne on one side and Bee on the other. I empty my rucksack out on the floor. Everyone dives on their stuff with thanks, until Felicity sees that I haven't brought back a *Guardian*.

"Excuse me, I can't see my paper in here, I can only see yours."

Of course she thinks I read the fucking *Daily Star*. "No, that's for you."

"But I asked you for a *Guardian*!"

"Oh, they didn't have any. Never mind, that one has more pictures in it."

She opens it up and immediately fakes an attack of the vapours. I don't know what she's making a fuss about, I think the woman has quite nice tits. Titania and Bee crowd round her to replenish her attention levels. To give Joanne and Fax their credit, they don't seem that bothered. I suspect Fax has seen her do this a million times. Joanne just wants her Maltesers.

I sit down and open a tube of Pringles, satisfied with my day's work so far. I offer them round but no one wants any. This is bad, it means I'm going to eat the whole tube.

"Ha," I say to Joanne. "I shouldn't be eating these. They're not going to like it at Slimming World." I eat three in one go.

"Excuse me."

At first it doesn't register that the 'excuse me' is aimed at me. I'm concentrating on eating my Pringles.

"Excuse me." This is accompanied by a tap on my arm. I jump a bit when I look up because Bee has teleported and is now right fucking next to me.

"Oh, sorry?"

"Excuse me, I find that really triggering."

"Sorry, what?"

"I said I find that really triggering, so you shouldn't talk about that."

Once again I start to wonder if there's something wrong with her. "Sorry, what are you talking about?"

Titania sticks her stupid uninvited nose in. "Oh come on, you know perfectly well what you said. You're deliberately using triggering, body-shaming language."

I'm so confused I forget to swallow my Pringle, so it's left half hanging out of my mouth.

Bee picks up Titania's growing anger and runs with it. Not literally, I doubt she can run. "You think that just because I'm a real woman with curves, you think you should sit there body shaming me? Pretending to be on a diet in front of me, just to make me feel bad?"

Ladies and gentlemen, we have entered *The Twilight Zone*. And by *The Twilight Zone*, I mean it's full of fat girls who love sparkly things.

I finally swallow my Pringle. I've managed to work out that it's something to do with her being fat. Then I panic. Did I accidentally say something like 'You're a whale with the brain of a six year old and it's a good job Fax doesn't want to have sex with you because you'd crush him'? I'm pretty sure I didn't say that. I look over at Joanne for reassurance, but she's having what looks like a staring contest with Fax.

"What did I say?"

"Oh that's right, make us repeat your hate speech."

Now Bee is eyeing my tube of Pringles. Maybe I forgot to offer her any? Maybe that's why she's suddenly upset?

"Do you want some Pringles?"

You'd think I just tried to punch her in the face. She rears up and starts sniffing in a weird sort of way. "Why are you being so horrible and triggering? You think that just because I have a real woman's body all I think about is food? I'll have you know I only eat to keep my blood sugars up!" With that she runs back to her tent at the approximate speed of one mile a year. Titania calls me a "body shaming Nazi" and goes after Bee. I still have no idea what's going on.

Felicity is, against all the odds, engrossed in her *Daily Star*, so she doesn't notice them go. Neither do Joanne and Fax. Fax has his hand up Joanne's jumper. I decide that what I'd like to do now is get into the tent and drink some booze out of Daniel O'Donnell, so that's what I do.

30. DANCING

Joanne tries and fails to knock on the tent flap, which results in her just pushing the flap in a bit. To make up for this she says "Knock knock. Look I'm knocking." I have no idea why she's trying to knock. Maybe she's worried I'm naked. If only she'd been that inhibited last night.

I try to answer her knock. "Come on." Oh shit I must be a bit pissed. "I mean come in."

Joanne comes in. "Are you ready or what?"

"Ready? What for?"

"God, *Music as the Hidden Talisman for Raising Your Vibrations!*"

"Hidden? What?"

"Chris' lute thing!"

Oh shit, I agreed to go to that earlier didn't I. Oh God why am I pissed? I have to sober up.

"Yeah two minutes…"

Brilliant idea – I'll eat the coffee I bought earlier. Coffee sobers you up. Fuck hot water, there isn't time. Shit, no, the coffee's outside and I'm inside. Right, act natural.

My foot catches on the tent as I'm climbing out and I fall on my head. Joanne laughs instead of doing anything useful like checking I'm not dead. At least she's not telling me off for being pissed, although to be fair I haven't tried to walk anywhere yet.

The coffee is where I left it, but when I grab my spoon it's still a bit sticky with varnish. Shit. Better not risk it. OK, what would a survival person with no spoons do? I try to imagine Bear Grylls doing one of his survival programmes. I like Bear Grylls. I think about Bear Grylls so much that I forget to think about the spoon problem. You know what, he'd probably just tip it into his mouth. I follow his example, but I misjudge the angle and I end up with more coffee in mouth than my mouth can actually hold. This amount of raw coffee might actually kill me. I'm starting to choke a bit.

Fax spots me dying of coffee and decides to come and do the Heimlich on me. I do spit out my coffee, but it also tickles and my reflex reaction is to nut him in the head. And now Fax is on the floor and Joanne is dancing around and shouting because she doesn't know what else to do and I still haven't sobered up.

It's OK because Fax sits up after a few seconds. Joanne would have been really cross if I'd killed him. She'd have pissed in every mug I own.

"Well, a fellow should not approach m'lady's hand-maiden from the back."

"Oh shit I'm really sorry, are you OK? I'm sorry I think you just got me in the ribs." This is what I mean to say, but it comes out sounding more like 'Shit you're my got ribs".

He lets me help him up so he's not mad at me. Joanne stops dancing and starts wibbling around next to Fax, gushing about how he saved my life. Meh. Right, Plan B – try to act sober. This will mostly involve not doing or saying anything for the rest of the evening, and trying not to fall asleep. I'm all over this.

Apparently Chris and the bitches from hell have gone

on ahead, so the three of us make our way to the 'Echoes of Pan' tent. Of course there's nothing as advanced as chairs in this tent – we all have to sit on the floor like it's a school assembly. Everyone's sitting in a circle round the edge of the tent, so I assume the stage bit is in the middle. I hope Chris hasn't been eating those 'bennies'.

Right, sitting. I can do that. We all plop onto the floor. I plop onto the floor more than the others. I think what might help sober me up is some more booze, so I take my bottle of vodka out of my bag. It's not full any more so it's sloshing around. Instead of shushing me and my bottle, Joanne and Fax demand to have some vodka. I'm relieved there's no one pretending to have diabetic fumes.

Speaking of which, shouldn't my mortal enemies be somewhere nearby? I do a quick scan of the tent and, to my delight, they're sat over on the other side. I wave my bottle at them, just so they notice me and don't worry that I'm missing. I'm confident they can't possibly start shouting made up rules at me in here. They scowl at me.

A woman with multicoloured hair appears in the middle of the circle. "Namaste." She does a little bow with her hands together. "Thank you for coming and sharing your consciousness at this performance event."

I hope this doesn't mean I've got to do anything. I yawn. Joanne prods me.

"Just a word before we begin. Obviously we discourage the use of mobile phones while the performance is manifesting. And in this tent, we like to show our appreciation by clicking our fingers or waving. We find applause to be rather disruptive of the vibrational manifestations that build up."

I think this means we shouldn't clap. It probably also means we shouldn't boo or shout advice to the performers. No word on whether singing along is acceptable.

"Our first performers tonight are a pair of musicians who interweave Celtic melodies to create an ambience suited to the more virile, masculine end of the crystal spectrum. This is ideally suited to obsidian and tiger's eye. However, the fans of rose quartz among us will still be able to attune to the higher wind overtones."

Nope.

"So without further ado, please send welcoming thoughts to Chris Pearson and Lara McFadden..."

Everyone starts waving and clicking. Chris is joined in the middle of the circle by the blondest woman I've ever seen. She looks like a Christmas ornament, and is playing some sort of whistle. The music is quite nice; it's the kind of stuff they sell on those CDs that have a picture of a forest on the cover.

Their first song stops and everyone starts waving their arms about. Some of the people forget they're holding crystals, and one of the crystals flies into the middle and hits the blonde woman on the arm. Its mortified owner rushes into the circle to retrieve it.

20 minutes later I'm getting very fidgety, and I'm starting to wonder how long it's going to go on for. I go to drink some vodka to find Joanne and Fax have nearly finished the whole fucking bottle. Chris and the blonde woman have been playing one long tune for the last 10 minutes. This stops, there's some more arm waving. The next tune makes me think there's some sort of pre-arranged etiquette to these things, because a load of people stand up and start what I can only loosely call 'dancing'. I saw Joanne after she'd eaten some illegal mushrooms once; she was doing something similar then. That was before she'd started clinging onto the lamppost.

Fax joins her, and soon the two of them are swaying in an alarming way. I don't know if it's the vodka or the vibrations manifesting. Joanne is doing moves I'm sure she's nicked from my Davina McCall exercise DVD, and Fax is... doing a *Scooby-Doo* dream sequence? I wonder if I can manage to sneak out while everyone's preoccupied.

I start shuffling away on my arse. I've gone maybe half a foot when I notice Bee is standing up at the other side of the circle, only she's not dancing. She's standing and glaring at Joanne and Fax, like a hill in a mood. Joanne and Fax don't notice this, of course. They don't seem to notice anything much when they're together. It would be quite nice if it weren't for the fact that I know what they sound like when they...

Don't make me come over there, brain.

And now Titania and Felicity are standing up, shooting looks at Joanne and Fax.

Chris and the Christmas ornament finish their current tune, and now convention has gone out of the window and people applaud. Oh, I guess it's OK to applaud when it's the last tune.

They're followed by a man and a woman, who are playing bongos and a harp. On purpose. It sounds pretty much how you'd expect. People are starting to mill out of the tent, the Witches of Eastwick are among them. Joanne and Fax don't notice that the music has changed – they're doing exactly the same strange aerobics dancing. I shuffle out of the tent on my arse.

I scoot along outside the tent, straight into some mud. Fucking brilliant. While I'm there I see Bee doing that weird sniffing again, flanked by Titania and Felicity. It hasn't occurred to me to stand up yet. I hear them crapping on:

"Don't cry darling, he's not worth it..."

"We didn't think he was that serious about her..."

"He'll get tired of her, there's nothing to her..."

"Yeah, she's just a stick with no personality, she's not a *real* woman like you…"

"And as for that moronic friend of hers… well, what does that say about her…"

Well, now I really, *really* don't like these three.

31. ART

Joanne and Fax are busy this morning, having more sex. I assume this is what they're doing because they've gone to find a rowan tree. This leaves me with two choices – hang around the tent minding my own business and getting a bit pissed, or throw myself on the mercy of the 'activities'.

Unfortunately, just as I'm settling down with a drink and a battered magazine of Joanne's, three shadows descend. They claim to be looking for Chris, to congratulate him on his performance last night. Chris pops his head out of the tent. He has a cigarette on the go, but strangely Felicity doesn't seem to notice. Maybe her diabetes has cleared up.

"Oh you clever thing! That concert was terribly good…"

This is my cue to leave. I don't care where I go as long as I don't have to sit there while they figure out which imaginary thing I'm doing to offend them today.

I take my bottle and head off. I'm not really sure what I'll do; I guess I'll find somewhere vaguely interesting and sit there. Half an hour later I'm settled under a tree (I don't think it's a rowan tree) with my drink and my magazine, and so far no one has bothered me. A jester has danced past a couple of times, but I don't feel any real need to chase him away with a big stick.

Of course my luck can't last – a couple park themselves a few feet away from me and start excitedly discussing a woman called 'Swallow' who does painting. I can deal with this as long as they don't start feeling any need to include me. Five minutes later they're joined by their friends – a man with the world's longest hair and his wife. I have to work to drown out their conversation about 'Swallow, she's so amazing' as I try to concentrate on an article called 'My dentist tried to bite my toes off!'. The woman in the article doesn't explain how her dentist managed to get her shoes and socks off without her noticing. I'm trying to figure out how he might have done this when three more people turn up and join in the 'Swallow and her imaginative art and she's so amazing' conversation. For fuck's sake. I'm starting to reach the limits of my naturally sunny personality.

They're not shouting like dicks or anything though, so I can kind of tune them out. I think he must have deliberately given her too much anaesthetic or something. She does say he injected her because she was having root canal, which does raise the question – didn't alarm bells ring in her head when he stopped poking around in her mouth and went to the other end? Either I'm pissed again or this article is bollocks. Or both.

A woman approaches the tree and says "Hi guys, I'm Swallow Rosen. It's so wonderful to see so many of you have turned up. We'll get started in a minute."

I look up and see with alarm that the chatting people have all gathered in a cross-legged group around me, which makes me included in this group by default. I feel like I'm being eaten by the Borg. And anyway, get started with what? What are they doing that I'm now going to have to do? Shit.

The Swallow woman starts unpacking a big canvas bag,

and brings out a load of paintbrushes. Oh of course, this is the artist woman. Fine, a painting class, no probs, I can do that. At least it isn't 'communicate with your kidneys' or 'naked gambling'. She hands round the brushes. I take one, thereby forfeiting any chance I had of standing up and going "Nope, sorry, you're all fucking weird" and running away.

I wait for her to get paints and stuff out, and start wondering how much all this is going to cost me. Or are we supposed to have brought our own paints? That would be a good excuse to not do it, even if it's a bit embarrassing. I look round but no one else has any painting gear; they're just looking at 'Swallow Rosen' (there's no fucking way that's a real name) and waiting for her next move.

"OK, find a space everyone."

This is one of my least favourite phrases, ever. 'Find a space' was something we had to do in PE when I was little. Our whole class, clad in vest and pants, would have to 'find a space' on the freezing hall floor, then spend 40 minutes pretending to be a tree, or an ice cream, or somewhere that wasn't in a big cold room wearing nothing but underwear. The boy I had a crush on wore racing car underpants. I wonder if Andrew Lincoln wears racing car underpants?

Everyone finds a space except me. Luckily this leaves me with plenty of space. I guess that's only fair since I was here first. I put my magazine away. Please God we're not going to have to paint with poo or blood or something.

"OK guys, my name is Swallow Rosen, and welcome to *Thought Painting*."

Everyone claps. By the time I've worked out that I should clap too, they've stopped clapping.

"OK, I see a lot of familiar faces here. And I see one or two new ones, so welcome all. As you know, thought painting is a wonderful, mind focusing activity, that negates the stress of perceived ability and competition with others…"

Yeah that's all very nice lady, but what is it we're supposed to paint on?

"…as my previous students know, I'm not a great proponent of lecturing – I believe in gently nudging you down the stream of learning…"

Canvas or paper or something? Any hints?

"So what I would suggest is getting started and seeing where it takes you. Remember, there is no right or wrong technique here…"

Back of a bus ticket?

"And I'll be coming round to guide you in the right direction. Any questions?"

I put my hand up. "What is it we're doing?"

The group laughs. I hate the group. I'm going to sneak into long haired man's tent tonight and cut all his hair off apart from one bit at the front. That'll show him.

"I'm sorry, what's your name my love?"

"Melissa. I…"

I was going to say 'I'm here by accident', but she cuts me off.

"Well I'm glad you've decided to try a new experience."

She smiles at me. I don't think she's taking the piss. Maybe if I drink some more of my vodka it'll be OK.

"And how much do you know about the class?"

The group are looking at me. I don't want them to laugh at me again.

"It's… painting?"

The group laughs. I'm going to beat them all to death with my magazine.

'Swallow' smiles at me. She has incredibly pointy teeth. "It is painting my love, but it's so much more than just painting. It's painting with your mind. It's painting with your thoughts, with your soul."

Right, that's that all explained.

She notes my look of confusion and comes to sit next to me. "Thought painting is an incredibly enriching mind experience. We take our brush -"

She takes my hand, which is holding my brush, and waves it around.

"– and create wonders of the mind. The world is your canvas, your imagination is your paint! You are the tool!"

I am the tool.

'Swallow' goes back to the front of the group. "Let's begin. I want you to paint a feeling. Close your eyes…"

I close my eyes, keeping one eye open.

"Close your eyes my love, we're visualising our picture."

I close my eyes and think about beating Titania to death with the engine from a Vauxhall Corsa. I open my eyes after 30 seconds because I'm bored and I'm still not entirely sure what we're supposed to be doing.

'Swallow' is sitting next to the man with the long hair. They're swaying together. From their conversation I can work out that we're just supposed to be imagining a picture, and that's literally all we're doing. Why did she give us paintbrushes? Long hair is telling her about his 'picture'.

"The ravine is so deep your soul is lost in it…"

Shit I hope she doesn't come and check on my 'picture'. I bet she does. If she goes in any sort of linear order I'm in trouble – there's only one person between me and long hair.

"The clouds are forming a brooding phallus…"

I better think of something good just in case. Although I'm not sure how I'm going to top 'brooding phallus'.

"And how does the ravine *feel* to be such a vessel of nothingness?"

Shit I can't think of anything. Whenever someone asks

me to think of something, I think of a happy childhood memory. I might as well start with that.

Before I can get my 'picture' together, 'Swallow' is looming over me, demanding to know what I'm 'painting'.

"Christmas shopping at Rumbelows."

What can I say, I panicked.

'Swallow' has clearly never heard of Rumbelows. What is she, a Martian? "Rumbelows was an electrical and electronics retailer in the United Kingdom, which once rivalled Currys, Dixons and Comet," I tell her, channelling the Wikipedia page for Rumbelows (I was pissed and lonely one night).

To help her, I start swaying like long hair guy. "You know, quality electricals at low low prices. I think there was a talking video recorder once…"

I glance at her and she's rubbing her temples. "Christmas, let's start with that. What I'd normally encourage people to paint is more of a… spiritual experience. Let's go with Christmas… how about a Yule scene?"

Yule? I know, that's like Yule logs. I've heard of Yule. Whenever I hear that word I picture it snowing on a Swiss roll.

"And what are you visualising now my love?"

"Snow on a Swiss roll."

She orders me to 'ground and centre' for five minutes then goes off to someone else.

I don't know what grounding and centring is, so I assume it's grinding my already muddy arse into the floor and getting all my things into one neat pile. Then I carry on thinking about Rumbelows. Only this time, I'm beating Titania to death with an Alba stereo. This makes me happy.

'Swallow' comes prowling round again, and I'm forced to tell her that now I'm visualising the smell of the carpet in Tandy. Then I have to tell her what Tandy is. I guess my parents took me to electrical shops a lot. Must be all the gear they bought for their gigs.

"That's not quite the purpose of this workshop my love."

I open my eyes again. "Oh dear."

"What we're really going for here is an inner manifestation of the art of the self."

"Right." I try again. "Erm, there's a tree?"

"Good, good! And what is that tree *telling* you?"

I desperately try to think of something spiritual to say. "It's saying... calm your tits."

She gets a bit annoyed with me. "I'm not sure this is really working out for you my love."

Thank God, this means I can go. "No, I think you're right. I probably shouldn't waste any more of your time."

With that I get up and wander back to the tent. Those three must have fucked off somewhere by now. I still can't figure out how that dentist did that.

32. CHATTING

Joanne and Fax are back from their sex expedition. Joanne informs me that they found a rowan tree, but there was a "selfish man eating an ice cream near it", so that bit of their plan was foiled. In the end they just came back and did it in Fax's tent. What I really want to do is put my hands over my ears to block out the sound of her telling me this, but I can't because that would be rude. To distract her I tell her about the thought painting.

"Oh I've done that! Isn't Swallow Rosen marvellous?"

Of course she's fucking done thought painting. It's exactly the sort of thing she'd become obsessed with for a week then never do again.

"Where's Fax anyway?"

"Oh, he's gone to a male bonding workshop."

"A what?"

"Yeah, he thinks it's unhealthy that he has so many female friends. I mean, even though he has such a positive feminine life force emanating from him, he has this idea that he should become more attuned to his inner hunter–gatherer."

"Right. So what is it he's gone to do?"

"They're making dream catchers I think."

Of course they are. I can't think of a single thing to do that's manlier, apart from reading *CROCHET GIRL!*.

"So do you want to do something?"

I know she's only asking me because Fax is busy. On the other hand, they did invite me to the spoon carving...

"Yeah I guess. What were you going to do?"

I expect her to say something like *The Plight of Tuna as Told Through Mosaic*, but to my relief she just says "I was just going to hang round here for a bit actually. I'm pretty tired."

I bet she is.

"That sounds lovely."

I start telling her about the thing I read in her magazine. "What I can't figure out is this – how did he get her shoes and socks off?"

Joanne thinks about this. "She wasn't necessarily wearing socks."

"You're missing the point a bit."

I rummage round in the tent looking for Daniel. The tent is now spectacularly messy. This is Joanne's fault, she's left fucking crystals, tarot cards and assorted shit lying around. I find Daniel under a copy of *Spirit And Destiny*.

"Hi Daniel, how have you been? I'm sorry we haven't had a chance to catch up for a bit."

Daniel smiles at me so I know he's not in a mood with me.

"Listen though Daniel," I whisper. "She's probably going to want to talk about having sex with Fax. We've got to try to head her off, OK?"

Daniel agrees.

To my amazement, Joanne just wants to talk about the festival. She doesn't mention Fax's 'essence', or the fact that he is a mountain lion. We have a good bitch about Titania, Felicity and Bee. I tell her about my Bee–friendzoned theory. She agrees with me.

"Oh I know. I mean, I feel a bit bad but what can I do about it? I mean, obviously I know how she feels, but she can't just expect me to stop going out with him."

I think this is the most sensible thing she's ever said.

"Fax doesn't have a clue about her though."

"He seems really nice."

It occurs to me that this is the first time we've been able to talk about Fax properly since we got here.

Joanne starts grinning. "Yes, I love him very much and he loves me very much."

Oh God. I'm happy for her but if this conversation turns into her telling me anything at all involving Fax's genitals then I'm going to kill myself.

"I wish you had a boyfriend, then it would all be perfect."

I shrug. I'm not that fussed about a boyfriend at the moment. The thought of having to do a relationship on top of everything else is a bit tiring.

"I know, you could go out with Chris!"

I have to get serious then. "Joanne, if you try to set me up with Chris I will set fire to you."

"God chill out, I mean he seems pretty nice."

So far my experience of Chris has been the following:

1. He watched us struggle with our tent then offered us a roll of Sellotape.
2. He plays the lute
3. He wears sunglasses at night
4. He sniffs poppers and eats those things he calls 'bennies'.

Possibly Chris is the last man on Earth I would want to go out with, apart from Fax. And anyway, I doubt Chris would want to go out with me. We have nothing in common. I don't play the lute, and he doesn't fancy

Andrew Lincoln.

Joanne lets the subject go, but instead she launches into a monologue about Fax and the poem he wrote for her. I think I'd rather talk about going on a date with Chris and his lute.

This is the poem that Fax wrote for Joanne:

THE DRAGON'S POWER

The dragon is wise
You have nice eyes
Thou art a wheel
In that thou art round and round
Wheel!
Thou art the parsley of my mind
With thy wings of black
And thy coat of splendour...

This goes on and on in the same vein. I'm not sure what it has to do with dragons. He gets a mention of her feet in there. Joanne seems to love it anyway. She does a bit of a swoon when she finishes.

"That was... nice."

"I know, Fax is such a genius. You can see why he turned down that Oxford professor job."

"Absolutely."

Despite all the crapping on about Fax and the fake things he's done, this is nice. I realise I've missed Joanne a bit. I do wonder why she's so willing to believe all this crap though. Probably best not to say anything. And it's not like Fax has said anything really bad. I mean, he's probably just trying to big himself up in front of Joanne. It's kind of sweet I suppose.

Speak of the devil –

"Hello m'lady."

"Fax!" Joanne jumps up and hugs him like she hasn't seen him for a year. "I missed you! How was your male bonding?"

"Fine."

"Just fine?"

Fax looks a bit apprehensive. "It wasn't what I expected."

"Oh no, how come?"

Fax sits down. "Well, I thought we were going to be making dream catchers. That's what the person who told me about it said."

Joanne starts rubbing his sleeve. This is becoming her signature move. "Oh no! So what did you end up doing?"

He pauses. "…male bonding… things"

"Like what?"

"Well… things that… only a man can do."

Joanne looks at me. I look at Joanne. Neither of us know what he's talking about.

"What did they make you do?"

"Well… we had to all stand round in a circle, and the theme was 'expressing the male energies'…"

"So what did you do in the end?"

Fax has gone the colour of beetroot. "Well, they encouraged us to…"

For fuck's sake, what did they do, murder someone?

"…release the male energies. Physically. Onto the floor."

He looks at Joanne. Joanne looks at him. I look at my nails.

Joanne is horrified. "God, did they make you do that in front of strangers?"

"Well yes, a bit. They said it would help us to become better attuned to our alpha male sides."

I think this might be a good time to leave Joanne and Fax to it. Poor Fax. Poor wanking Fax.

33. BASH

Joanne is comforting Fax in the tent. I am outside the tent re-reading this dentist article. I still can't figure out how he did it without her noticing. Maybe I'll email the magazine and ask them. What's important is that I get no more information about Fax and his wanking circle.

It's starting to get dark. Right on cue, Chris emerges from his tent and puts his sunglasses on. I can't take it any more.

"Why do you only wear sunglasses in the dark?"

"Oh, I believe we respond better to the extremes of nature, so when it's dark I think it should be, like, really dark."

That's a good enough explanation I guess. At least he isn't offended.

"Anyway, I need to do something, I've had some bennies. What's going on?"

Oh God he's had those weird awake–but–shitting pills. I should tell a policeman but there aren't any policemen here, just men in hi-vis vests. Maybe I should tell one of them? No, I can't be fucked with walking all that way. I'll wait and see if he kills anyone first.

Before I can think of an excuse for us having to move

tents, Joanne and Fax appear. Fax still looks a bit upset, but Joanne is bouncing.

"Yo, Chris! Are you partying with us tonight?"

I suspect Joanne wants Chris to make friends with Fax so he won't feel the need to do public wanking in the name of male bonding.

"Party? Yes ma'am."

"Yeah we're all getting round the fire for a party in a bit."

"Sweet."

Now Joanne and Fax are out I can have a bit of a sleep in the tent. I wake up to Joanne prodding me:

"Yo, we're going over there."

"What? Where?"

"God, over to Fax's tent! Are you coming or what?"

"Yeah hang on."

Oh shit I've just agreed to go spend time with those three. I assume they're going to be there. I assume Bee has to see Fax every half an hour or she'll kill herself.

Fax has got another fire going. I hope he's not going to cook any more savoury orbs. I suppose this is going to be our 'last night bash'. It's gone bloody quick, but I can't act anything other than relieved to be going home tomorrow.

The Witches of Eastwick are sat round in a huddle again. I don't even bother saying hello to them. Fuck it, it's not like I'm ever going to have to spend any time with them ever again. I park myself next to Chris, who is examining a bag of pills. I wonder if these are the 'bennies' he's been talking about?

"Yo, do you want one of these?"

"No I'm OK thanks."

His leg seems to be shaking on its own. It's very distracting. He starts rambling on about army reservists. I turn my attention to Joanne and Fax, who are discussing something called 'energy medallions'. I'm fucked if I know what they're talking about. Brilliant. A choice between listening to a conversation about 'energy medallions' and listening to Chris grind his teeth and talk about how he's going to join the army tomorrow.

After a while Chris goes off to the loo. He leaves his bag of pills behind. As soon as he's out of sight, Felicity makes a beeline for the bag and takes a few pills out.

"What are you doing? They're Chris's."

She looks at me like I said 'I just shit in your tea'. "Yes well he's not going to miss a few is he?" She rolls her eyes.

"Well, that's not really the point."

She tuts. "Look, just mind your own business. He isn't going to miss a couple of Valium."

I'm almost certain those aren't Valium. I don't know much about drugs, but I know that Valium is supposed to relax you, not make you really, really awake and then make you shit yourself.

I should probably tell her she's mistaken. I really should tell her. I don't tell her.

By the time Chris gets back I've conveniently forgotten that Felicity has stolen some of his pills.

"Fucking hell man I've got to lay off the bennies."

"What? Oh those, yeah you probably should."

"Yeah man I'd hate to be me in the morning. My fucking guts."

I can't believe Joanne suggested I go out with this man. My mind drifts into a nightmare scenario in which I'm married to Chris. Since I don't really know much about him, our entire marriage revolves around Sellotape, lute music and me never being able to use the bathroom because he's constantly in there shitting himself.

This horrible fake marriage is poked out of my mind by Joanne, who announces that she's going to sleep in

Fax's tent tonight.

This reminds me. "Fax, can I see your tattoos please? I've seen them on a photo and I meant to ask you about them."

"Of course." He stands up and starts unbuttoning his trousers.

"No no, just the ones on your arms I meant."

"Oh, OK then."

The wolves howling at the moon one is as stupid as I remember, but what I'm really interested in is the 'Jason Donovan' one. Is it Jason Donovan? It can't be, but it really, really looks like him.

"Who's that?"

"That's my brother Guy. He's abroad. He lives in Toronto."

I really, really want to comment on how much he looks like Jason Donovan, but I can't in case the real Guy looks nothing like Jason Donovan and then I'd be saying his tattoo was rubbish. Also, why does he have a tattoo of his brother, who is apparently alive and well and living in Canada?

"And next I'm going to get a tattoo of m'lady."

Joanne grins at him. "And I'm going to get a tattoo of Fax."

With zero warning, Bee stands up and yells at Joanne: "Just leave him alone you skinny bitch!"

No one speaks. No one moves.

"Fax, how could you do this to me?"

Fax looks bemused.

"I've always been there for you Fax, why can't you look past my curves and see that we're meant to be together? I'm not going to let you waste your life with this... bag of bones!"

"I... what?"

"You know I'm in love with you Fax. And I know that you love me, deep down. How can you not think we're supposed to be together?"

Joanne stands up. "I've had enough of this. Stop trying to nick Fax off me you fucking mental whale!"

Bee lunges at Joanne. I think what follows is technically a fight, but I'm not sure. There's a lot of hair pulling and nipping. At one point Joanne attempts to give Bee a Chinese burn. Titania and Felicity are shouting stuff at Joanne and Fax:

"Fax how could you! What, so Bee isn't good enough for you?"

"Leave her alone you body shaming cow!"

"Why can't you see that Bee's a *real* woman?"

I might as well join in. "Shut up you pair of twats!"

The fight breaks up when Joanne threatens to "stick a tent pole up your arse!" Bee thunders away and hides in her tent. Titania and Felicity go and sit outside the tent, saying encouraging bullshit through the canvas. Joanne and Fax go off to his tent. I guess the party's winding down then.

Chris taps me on the shoulder. "Did they just have a fight?"

What fucking planet is he on.

"Yes. Over Fax."

"Why? Does that one want to go out with Fax as well then?"

"What? Did you nod off or something?"

He thinks for a minute. "Maybe."

"Well, yeah, she says she's in love with him. Mind you, I saw this coming. It was obvious."

Chris puts his sunglasses back on. "That's a shame. I was thinking I might make a move. I like curvy women. She has fantastic tits. Oh well."

Before I can think of a reply that doesn't include 'Eew you mental bastard', he stands up and heads back towards his tent. I should probably go too. I stare into the fire for five minutes before I can be arsed to move. It's been a tiring day, what with thinking about Rumbelows and sitting here watching fights. And tomorrow we've got to somehow figure out how to get the tent back into the box.

34. BUS, PART 2

I'm in the best mood I've been in for a while. This is because we're finally on our way home. God I've missed civilization. Joanne is depressed because she's been prised away from Fax. They clung to each other this morning like those novelty cruets you get at Argos. There was lots of talk about feelings and shit, and they promised to get on Skype the minute they both got home. I can already see what that's going to be like. Joanne's going to sit snivelling into the webcam while I'm trying to watch TV.

The slightly awkward thing is that we've got to go back on the 'Goddess Empowerment' bus, which we are sharing with Titania and Felicity. Thank God, Bee has made alternative arrangements. They're sitting two seats in front of us, but I can still feel the hate radiating from them. It's a pity I've run out of booze, because I would happily have drunk it all on the bus just to make Felicity have another fake panic attack.

I can hear their conversation. Maybe that's because I'm now attuned to Titania's horrible whiny voice. So far they haven't slagged us off. If they do I'll start throwing stuff at them.

"I took those Valium, but I couldn't get to sleep at all."

"Are these the pills you borrowed from the drug addict?"

"Yeah. I mean, I was doing him a favour really wasn't I?"

"Yeah you were. And it's not like he'd have ever noticed!"

Hoots of laughter.

"My stomach feels a bit off this morning though."

I do a quick calculation in my head. We have about three hours left of this journey. If I've understood their conversation correctly, Felicity had some of Chris' 'bennies' last night, and is now due a bout of explosive diarrhoea. When I consider the implications of this, I'm not sure whether to burst out laughing or try to jump out of the moving bus. It's like waiting for a bomb to go off.

Joanne's dozing. I prod her awake.

"What? Are we back?"

"No, listen…"

I whisper the situation to her. Her eyes widen in horror. "Oh my god she's had bennies? Jesus, you shouldn't have those. Chris is hard and he's used to them I guess. I had one once. Never again."

"He kept offering me one."

"I'm glad you said no. Oh God she's gonna shit on the bus…"

"She thought they were Valium."

"They look fucking nothing like Valiums. I think Valiums are pointy."

We observe Felicity for about fifteen minutes. Noth--ing seems to be happening. It's like watching a science experiment. Then Titania pipes up with "Can you smell something?"

Felicity leaps up and yells to the driver: "Stop! Stop the bus! I have to get off RIGHT NOW!"

"I can't stop here Flick, it's the motorway! There are services in ten miles…"

"FUCKING STOP THIS BUS NOW PAULA! I'M 100% SERIOUS! I WILL NOT BE RESPONSIBLE FOR –"

She stops shouting and clutches her stomach. Now it really stinks on this bus, and it isn't just B.O.

Five minutes later, the bus is sitting on the hard shoulder. There's a bit of a jam; the cars are crawling past us. Felicity is outside the bus, pooing on the ground. Not that I'm looking or anything. The people driving past are looking though.

35. HOMECOMING

Something's different about the house. I can't quite put my finger on it. I'm sure I'll get it if I give it enough thought.

We've only just stopped laughing. Three solid hours of sitting in a minibus sniggering and shushing each other has taken it out of us. The others on the bus weren't laughing. They just looked ill.

Something's definitely different. What is it?

Joanne dumps the tent box in the garden and fumbles for her keys. "OK I need to go on Skype so I need the living room."

Can't she wait until we get through the fucking door to start ordering me out of the living room?

I look at the door. It's the door, there's something different about it. I –

"Jo, didn't we used to have some numbers on our house?"

She looks up from rummaging in her bag. "What? Oh yeah you're right we did."

Someone's stolen our numbers off our house. I'm sure there used to be a '4' and a '9' there. We peer through the window to check we've definitely got the right house. Joanne's bong is on the living room floor, along with that pan of water that I really need to clear away.

Whoever it was, I don't think they even tried to break in. The house looks exactly as it did when we left, except now it has no numbers. Someone needed those exact numbers so urgently that they stole them off our door? This is really confusing.

"I guess they just needed some numbers." She shrugs. Fucking Sherlock Holmes.

"Should I... phone the police?"

"What? I'm not a grass. Anyway shut up I'm trying to find my keys, I have to get on Skype."

I'm not sure how reporting a theft is considered being a grass. To be fair though, if I told the police we'd had our numbers nicked, they'd probably just go "So?"

We get in and dump our stuff. I don't know where the Avon Deluxe is going to live now. I do know that I will never be using it ever fucking again.

I've missed our house. I get a mad urge to sniff the carpet and the settee. I settle for putting the kettle on.

"Do you want a cup of tea?"

"Shhhh!"

I look back into the living room. Wow, she doesn't hang about. She's already got her laptop on.

I hear the laptop say "Hello m'lady, I've missed thou..."

I guess she's there for the evening then. I take my tea and my pile of unopened mail and head upstairs. Bill, bill, junk mail. Is this a card? I open the envelope and take out what I believe is called a 'notelet'. The words 'Thank You' are written on it in gold swirl:

Melissa,
I suppose you thought your wedding present was really funny. It's almost like you couldn't be bothered to get us a proper present and just wrapped up the first thing you saw

at the shops! Have you got any idea how embarrassing it was opening a pile of books? And I don't even know who two of them are! No wonder you ran off early. Your mum says she's really disappointed in you, and so she should be. To think your mum got us a Nespresso. I said to her...

She didn't like the autobiographies then.

36. UNCLE JEFF, PART 3

Right, I have to get this story straight in my head. I've been to a funeral, which lasted four days because apparently Greek people do that. Also I am now Greek.

Must not mention festivals, tents, or savoury orbs. Must stick to talking about my poor Uncle Jeff, or ideally, not talking at all. Jeff's not a very Greek name. Oh God I don't even know any Greek people.

I'm almost tempted to never go into work again so I don't have to carry on doing this lie. I'm no good at lying. I say the first thing that comes into my head and now look where it's got me. I should have at least googled 'Greek funerals'. I hope to God Karen hasn't done that, because there's no fucking way they last four days. I was going to google it last night, but I forgot and ended up playing 17 games of Freecell instead.

Well at least I don't look like I've been on holiday. People who get back off holidays are supposed to look all brown and happy. When I looked in the mirror this morning I had the complexion of a used bus ticket. Camping does not agree with me.

It's my turn to open up today, so at least I won't have to face Karen for another few hours. When I get in the shop there's a note on the counter:

> *Mel,*
> *Hi love, I'm not in today, hospital appt. Will ring later.*
> *Hope you're OK*
> *Karen xx*

I'm so relieved I accidentally take a Twix from the display and eat it.

The rest of the day passes without incident. Even though I'm at work, it's still a nice novelty to be back around electricity and floors and lightbulbs.

The phone rings. I answer without thinking –

"Hello, Co-op?"

"Hi love it's Karen. Did you get my note?"

Shit. Now she's going to test me on my lies. Quick, think of some funeral stuff just in case.

"Hi, yeah I did thanks. Everything's fine here."

"How was it? Your uncle, I mean…"

"Oh it went off without a hitch. Everyone got hammered."

I probably shouldn't have said that bit.

There's a pause. "Oh well, as long as it was a good send off."

"Yeah it was brilliant."

I really should not have called it 'brilliant'.

"Anyway, are you OK? You said you had a hospital appointment?"

"Oh, yeah just a gynaecologist thing. But I'm seeing the specialist in Stafford so I won't be back."

"That's fine, don't worry about it."

She goes then. She didn't sound suspicious. I'm sure she's more bothered about her fanny at the moment anyway. She probably hasn't given Uncle Jeff a second thought.

37. CARROT STICKS, PART 2

I'm not spending much time in the house, because Joanne refuses to move from the living room. She is more or less permanently Skyping with Fax. I have to remember not to walk in front of the laptop in my knickers because Fax will be able to see me. Also I can't have a drink then fall asleep on the living room floor. This is really inconvenient.

"Oh, my soul is withering away without you."

They hung out for four fucking days.

"It's OK because we're still quantumly entangled. Did you get a headache last night? Because I got part of your headache I think."

"Wow yes, yes I did! Wow you're so clever Fax."

"I do get sympathy pains sometimes. Like the time I had to deliver that woman's baby in the middle of Brantano..."

This is why I'm not spending much time in the house. I've been walking round the park, which isn't something I'd normally do but it's better than sitting in my room or listening to Fax lie about stuff he's done. Anyway it's quite nice in the park, and it's probably burning some calories. Sometimes I pass a group of people in pyjamas waving their limbs about. I think this is called 'Tai Chi'. I think Fax does that. He fucking would.

Tonight, though, I'm queuing up to get weighed again. I'm pretty much resigned to the fact that I'm going to reach 38 stone eventually, and that I should probably stop coming to Slimming World before I break their scales. Waste of fucking money anyway.

"Congratulations Melissa! Two and a half pounds lost this week!"

What? No fucking way. Ooh, that's quite good. Must be the fresh air or something. I wasn't going to stay to 'Image Therapy', but I think I will now, just to see what it's like to get applause that isn't from pity.

"Oh dear, Laura's gained a pound this week…"

Ha. Good. That'll teach her to be thinner than me.

"Kate has lost a pound!"

Fuck off Kate, stop trying to upstage me.

"Melissa has lost two and a half pounds. I think we can all agree that, after her shaky start, this is brilliant! Melissa, this also means that you're slimmer of the week!"

Marianne hands me a sticker. Everyone applauds. I'd quite like to get up and give a speech but they don't normally do that here. I've got a sticker though, which is the important thing. I am the fucking king of stickers now.

"Right ladies, today we're going to be looking at yummy Fakeaways!"

Unless these 'Fakeaways' involve lard, they're probably not going to be yummy. But since I'm a bit of a Teacher's Pet tonight, I should probably try to pay attention.

"…As you know ladies, boiled rice is completely free on Slimming World. What I would say though is be careful not to overdo it. About half a cup is the amount we recommend, which leaves plenty of room on your plate for piling up those lovely, healthy veggies!"

I fucking knew it.

"And of course, homemade curries can be a lot tastier

than ready-made ones, and they're so much better for you. For example, in the Slimming World magazine this month there's a delicious recipe for a spicy broccoli Masala, which takes no time at all..."

Nope, I'm still not convinced. No curry I've ever had has included broccoli.

Kate is making notes in her notebook, the fucking swot.

"Now, I want to briefly touch on the topic of fast food. While it's not strictly speaking takeaway food, it is quick and convenient for a lot of people. As slimmers, we must be extra careful when faced with a restaurant like McDonald's..."

I'm sure she looks at me when she says this. Fuck her, I've got a sticker.

"Now, we all know that French fries are a quick and cheap 'fill–you–up', but they're also not slimming friendly! So I want to get a few ideas going for what we could order instead, if we really *have* to get something from McDonald's..."

Someone puts their hand up. "They do salads don't they."

"Yes that's right! So you see ladies, there's really no reason why you'd have to order a yucky, greasy burger or fattening fries. Simply order one of their quick and easy salads! And of course, McDonald's has really been trying to expand the variety in their menu in recent years. For example, as well as yummy salads, did you also know that you can order carrot sticks?"

I'm going to buy one of those novelty keyrings that plays a fanfare when you press a button. I'm going to bring it to the next meeting, and I'm going to press it whenever she mentions carrot sticks. Maybe I could arrange for some balloons to fall on her head as well? I probably won't do that though. If I'm perfectly honest, I probably won't buy the keyring either.

As we're standing up to leave, Marianne shouts "Oh, I almost forgot! Before you go ladies, I have a super slimming drink recipe for you!"

We're ordered to sit down again as Marianne gives us a leaflet each:

Did you know there are two whole syns in just 25ml of Pimms? But don't worry – here's a recipe for summery, tasty, non-alcoholic Pimms! Simply take two tablespoons balsamic vinegar, add to lemonade, then serve with cucumber for that fresh taste of the summer!

I stare at the leaflet. OK, let me see if I've got this right. Marianne wants us to drink lemonade with vinegar in it, and that will somehow be the same as getting pissed on Pimms?

I check it again. Nope, that's right, she actually means for us to put vinegar in lemonade. And then to drink it. On purpose.

38. GUEST

I'm knackered tonight. Work was a pain because Karen has decided, for no real reason, that we should swap all the shelves around.

"We'll be getting the Christmas stuff in soon. I think it would be good if it has its own section. I was thinking about moving the baking stuff, but you know, Christmas, baking…"

"Mmm."

I stayed up too late last night. I was going to go to bed but they were selling a thing on QVC, so I stayed up and watched them selling it. I can't even remember what it was now.

"So I thought we could put the cleaning stuff at the back and that will free up some space…"

"Mmm."

So I spent the day moving bottles of Cillit Bang to the back of the shop. I have a bastard headache and I'm looking forward to going to bed. I don't think I'm even going to watch any QVC. I'm not even sure when I started watching QVC. I think I must have been pissed one night. And now I find myself watching it on purpose. Not that I'd ever buy anything from QVC. Probably.

When I get back Joanne is in the living room. So is Fax. So is all Fax's stuff.

"Surprise!"

I look around and then I edge back out of the room, closing the door behind me. I've seen them do this on TV. Sometimes, if you try coming into the room again, you'll find that you just imagined the thing you thought you saw. It barely ever works, but this might be one of the times it does work.

This is not one of those times.

Joanne acts like I didn't already come into the living room and go back out.

"Surprise!"

I look round the room again. There's nowhere to sit.

"Fax is moving in with us!"

"I…"

Nope, I'm drawing a blank.

I plaster a smile on my face. "Hang on, I've just got to… do something." I head into the kitchen and close the door behind me.

Fax has moved in. Fax moved into this house while I was at work. OK, don't panic.

I open the kitchen cupboard. I fucking knew it – Daniel has been hiding in there instead of keeping watch.

"Daniel how could you let this happen!"

He smiles, but it does not reassure me or win me over. In fact, it just looks like he's taking the piss.

"DANIEL YOU WERE SUPPOSED TO BE FUCKING KEEPING WATCH! THIS IS YOUR FAULT THIS HAS HAPPENED! WHAT ARE WE GOING TO DO ABOUT THIS?

Joanne comes in. "Who are you shouting at? Are you shouting at that cup?"

Everything's OK, don't panic. There's bound to be a

really simple solution to all this. Maybe I misheard her about Fax? I turn to face Joanne.

"Yes I am shouting, but I am not necessarily shouting just at Daniel. I'm probably just shouting near him."

"What? Are you OK?"

"What was that you said about Fax?"

She grins. "He's moving in!"

"That's what I thought. And is he moving in forever?"

"Yeah!"

"I see. I just have to pop out for five minutes."

I've never been to our local on my own before. We don't really come in here much at all, apart from to watch the fights at chucking out time. It's an old man's pub, with brown furniture and walls, and a fruit machine.

I head straight for the bar.

"Hello can I have a drink please."

The barman looks at me. "Um, do you know what you want?"

"What? Oh, I don't know, a big gin."

"House double?"

"Yes, three of those. Thank you."

He's dying to ask me what the matter is. I'm dying to tell him, or anyone, just to reassure myself that I'm not overreacting. But he doesn't ask me, and I don't offer any information. It's a weird stand-off that's only broken when I go sit at a table, neck one of the gins in one go then stare into space.

OK, don't panic.

No, I have to panic. There's no alternative. Joanne has moved her boyfriend of two fucking weeks into our house. His stuff is everywhere. He's going to use the toilet and play his acoustic guitar on a morning. They're going to have sex. Oh my god, they're going to have loads of sex. I'm never going to be able to go into my own house ever again.

I get some more gins. I should probably slow down a bit, but it's only half an hour to closing, so I don't have time to slow down. These old men in here don't know how lucky they are. They don't have Joanne and Fax in their house forever and ever. It's OK though – I've got a plan, and that plan consists of getting a bit hammered then thinking about this in the morning.

40 minutes later, the nice barman helps me home. I try to tell him about the numbers being stolen off our door, but I can't make the words come out right. Joanne answers the door.

"God, where did you go!"

"I had to... nip."

"I'm afraid she's had a few," says the nice barman.

I shove myself through the door and wave to the nice barman. "Thanks Bra-Man!"

Joanne closes the door then stands looking at me like an angry parent. "Why didn't you say you were going to the pub? We'd have come with you!"

"Fax lives here!" For some reason this is hilarious now.

"Yes I told you, he's moved in with us."

This is too much. I fall over in a fit of giggles. Upstairs, I hear Fax flushing the toilet.

39. SETTLING IN

This is fucking unbearable. Joanne and Fax have taken over the living room and I'm not allowed in it. OK, I suppose technically that's not true. But they have. And now being in my own house is like muscling in on a permanent date with them.

This morning they decided to do 'rage yoga' together. I'm used to Joanne doing it, but I can't be in there while Fax is doing it in those shorts. It's one thing to accidentally see Joanne's bits, but... in fact no, it is just as bad seeing Joanne's bits. I had to put up with the pair of them shouting "fucking wanker" at each other while I tried to watch some of last night's *Panorama*.

When they're not doing shit like that, they're either chanting or having sex. The other night they shared a bong and then did it up against her bedroom wall. I couldn't concentrate on my *Beano*. I'm going to have to confront her soon.

The problem is I'm not sure how to do that. I've never seen her so happy. She's stopped doing her 'dead fish' thing, and she's stopped getting in a state and trying to kick herself in the fanny. So that's a bonus. Plus, Fax is now paying a third of the rent, so he's saving me some money.

Given this, I have no idea how to go about demanding that Joanne kicks him out.

I've started showing up early to work. Karen's noticed, but I can't tell her about anything to do with the festival, so I just have to say that Joanne's moved her boyfriend in.

She tutted when I first told her. "That's typically inconsiderate of the girl. Didn't she even ask you?"

"No, she thought it would be a lovely surprise for me."

She raises an eyebrow. I wish I could do that. "And was it a lovely surprise?"

I hesitate. "…It was a surprise anyway."

Karen gives me a look. "Look I know she's your friend, but I have to be honest here, I can't for the life of me think why you put up with her."

I shrug. "We have a laugh together."

"And what kind of bloody name's Fax anyway?"

"It's not his real name. I don't know, something to do with fire or something."

"Well look it's really not on, what she's doing."

I'm not telling Karen to fuck off in my head so much at the moment, mostly because I agree with her. I still wish she'd fuck off a bit though.

I shrug again. "Yeah well… they're not doing anything really that bad I suppose."

"You're a bloody pushover sometimes, you know that?"

"Well what am I supposed to do? She's convinced she'll die if she's apart from him for half an hour. And to be fair he is paying rent, so…"

"So now you have no rights in your own house?"

"Yo, guess what!"

We both look towards the door and see Joanne and Fax standing there. Karen rolls her eyes. "Oh my god. Right I'm off in the back. Try not to let her keep you too long. *Stinking the bloody place out,*" she adds under her breath.

"We're having a party!"

I'm less than impressed by this proposal. "What sort of party?"

"A housewarming!"

"But we moved in two years ago."

"God, a late housewarming then. Where's Nick?"

"He's not in till later. *You're not inviting Nick.*"

"What, because he's black?"

"What? No, because I work with him, dickhead. I don't want you and Fax having sex while my colleagues are in the house."

She tuts. "Whatever. I'm going to invite him anyway. A party will do us both good. Plus I want to welcome Fax to the neighbourhood."

I'm not going to get a say in this at all. "For fuck's sake Jo, you never –"

There's a crash from the back of the shop. Me, Joanne and Karen all get there at the same time, and see Fax sitting in a pile of cans and assorted pop.

"I'm sorry, I was trying to get one without touching them. I can do that sometimes."

OK, fist in mouth time again. Joanne is doing her crisis dancing, and Karen is yelling at Fax:

"What the hell are you talking about? You're paying for all this or I'm calling the police!"

Joanne starts shouting at Karen: "Stop oppressing him, he's injured! And he used to work for NASA so he knows what he's talking about!"

Karen turns to me. "I'm really sorry Mel, but I'm going to have to bar these two for a bit."

Fax starts crying. I try to tell Karen that I'll get a mop, but I can't because if I take my fist out of my mouth I will explode. I nod and turn my back to them. Luckily, Joanne just thinks I'm really upset on Fax's behalf, so she doesn't go off on one at me. She helps Fax up.

"You still have to pay for the spoiled ones!"

Karen is blocking their way. I really wish I could help but I can't take my fist out of my mouth yet.

"Fine, God!" Joanne pulls another £50 note out of her bag. Where the hell is she getting these £50 notes? "Use it for your capitalism!"

Karen just takes the money. Joanne and Fax leave with as much dignity as possible, considering he's covered in pop and still crying a bit. As soon as they're gone, all the laughing comes out of me at once. Karen sees this and can't help joining in.

"Oh my god you live with them…"

This sentence makes me laugh less hard.

40. COOKERY

Fax has recovered from his ordeal at the Co-op. For a 'black belt ex-NASA genius who regularly wins fights with Steven Seagal', he's surprisingly sensitive. Joanne has "applied lavender oil to his base chakras", so he will apparently be fine.

We're sitting round not doing much. For once they're not doing some weird shit, so we can hang out together. I don't mind them when they're like this, it's just when they're having sex and singing folk songs that I can't stand to be around them.

They're still insisting on having this party. "I'll do my savoury orbs," says Fax.

"God you're such a brilliant cook," says Joanne.

I don't say anything, but I make a mental note to buy normal food, like anything else at all that I can find.

"That reminds me," says Fax. Did I ever tell you about my Reiki cookery?"

"Ooh, no!"

"Yeah, you can cook stuff just using reiki energy, and you don't need a cooker at all."

I suspect that's wrong.

"I can make my hands go really hot with the energy. I

cooked an egg once."

OK, of all Fax's made up stuff, 'I can cook an egg with magic powers' is up there at the top.

Joanne's doing her usual thing of just believing his bullshit. I don't know why she never calls him out on it. Either she actually believes half the stuff he says, or he's so good at sex that…

I'm warning you, brain. Stop that right now.

"Have you got an egg?"

Oh my god is he actually offering to give us a demonstration of his rubbish magic powers? I have to see this. I bet we haven't got an egg, but I'm going to get an egg if it kills me. I offer to go buy some eggs.

"Brill thanks. Ooh can you get me some Rizlas as well please?"

Great, eggs and Rizlas. I bet the Queen goes to the shop for eggs and Rizlas.

I wouldn't offer to go except there's a shop on the next street. We don't normally buy stuff from this shop because when you go in there the guy behind the counter stares at you until you leave. But this time I am determined. I nearly get Freddos, but at the last minute I remember that I've lost a bit of weight this week, so I don't. I hope this isn't the beginning of a downward spiral that will ultimately see me putting a carrot stick in my mouth and eating it, on purpose.

When I get back Joanne has lit an incense stick. Apparently this is to "align Fax's meridians properly". Fax is sitting cross legged on the floor.

"I got these ones. They're not free range…"

I am not spending an extra fucking quid on free range eggs just so Fax can spoil them with his bullshit.

"Oh that's OK, all eggs absorb energy the same I think."

Oh God he's actually going to try and do this. I fully

expected him to try and get out of it by saying he had a bad back or something.

"OK I need silence for this…"

We sit in silence while Fax holds an egg. Of all the things in the world we could be doing right now, we're choosing to sit in silence watching Fax hold an egg.

He starts doing some disturbing humming. It occurs to me that I'm spending a lot of time trying not to laugh recently. I suppose that's a step up from wishing I was dead.

"Aaaaaaaaaaaaa!"

Maybe if I try really hard, I can train myself to laugh out of my arse so he won't notice.

It's been about six or seven minutes now. He stops humming. "Ta da!"

He's still just sitting holding the egg. The egg hasn't changed.

"It's done now I think."

"Joanne gets in for a closer look. "Wow really?"

"Yes I think so. It's had a lot of energy. The ions in it have definitely changed."

I run to the kitchen to get a plate. Daniel looks at me curiously, but I'm not really speaking to Daniel at the moment. I haven't completely forgiven him for not stopping Fax moving in while I was out.

"Look just give me some time Daniel. That was a bad thing you did."

I put the plate down in front of Fax. He cracks the egg onto it. The egg plops out. Joanne peers at it.

"Is it soft boiled?"

"Yes."

The obviously raw egg sloshes round on the plate as Joanne examines it. "Wow. Can I eat it? I've never had a Reiki egg before."

Oh God I've got to say something now. "Jo, I wouldn't…"

They look at me.

"I'm not sure it's cooked… properly."

"Oh it definitely is," says Fax. "That's how the last one came out."

"And did you eat the last one?"

"Yeah."

"And you didn't get ill or anything."

"No, not from the egg."

Before I can say anything else, Joanne has grabbed the plate and tipped the whole egg into her mouth.

Her face goes funny. She almost looks as if, I don't know, as if she's eating a raw egg. To her credit, she swallows it. This is not going to end well.

"That… you know what I'm not sure it tasted like it was supposed to."

She looks at Fax. Her face has gone a bit green. I've never eaten a raw egg, but I can imagine it's not the most pleasant experience.

"No that's the energy that makes it taste funny."

"Oh."

Great. If Karen starts doing small talk tomorrow and asks me what I did last night, I'll have to say "I sat there while Joanne ate a raw egg after Fax held it for seven minutes." No wonder she thinks Joanne's a bad influence on me.

41. MYSTERY

I've never found out what Fax is supposed to do for a living. I guess he had a job that he packed in when he moved up here, but when I ask him about it he just says "Oh, I toiled for currency," then starts crapping on about his poetry. This always leads to him trying to recite the poetry to me, so I've stopped asking him.

He's helping Joanne with her 'work' now. They sit in the living room and chant, and ring bells, and then Joanne sends an email to her 'clients' asking for £100. I'm almost tempted to get in on this scam, except I can't call it a scam to Joanne's face, because she doesn't think it is.

I want to know what it is she thinks she does, so I ask her while Fax is in the bath and we're sat sharing a bottle of wine.

"What is your actual official job title?"

"God I've told you this loads of times!"

"Yeah I know but I've probably been pissed each time you've told me. Or I wasn't listening."

She rolls her eyes. "I'm a lightworker and vibrational practitioner."

"Right. And is that what Fax does as well?"

"Well he does a bit but he's much more into poetry. He

sometimes helps out at his friend's healing retreat."

"And what's that?"

"It's at his house in Doncaster. He runs spiritual awakenings and vibrational awareness weekends."

"And where did he work before he came up here?"

She rolls her eyes again. "God you're obsessed with what people do for money!"

"I'm not – I wouldn't have to keep asking if you'd fucking tell me!"

A thought passes through my mind. "Oh God was it something really embarrassing? Was he a stripper?"

The thought of Fax as a stripper immediately lets me know that he wasn't a stripper. You would not hire a stripper with a Jason Donovan tattoo. I down the wine in my glass.

She tuts and reaches for the bottle. "This is nearly empty. I know, we should go to the pub."

"Stop avoiding my question. What did Fax do for a living?"

"God it's really unfair to judge someone on their job you know."

I look at her. She fiddles with her lighter.

"He was in… advertising."

"What, an advertising agency, or he sold it, or…"

"…"

"…"

"For fuck's sake, he was Larry the Chicken Leg OK?"

My face is an expressionless mask.

"Anyway, he left after a disagreement. The owner was trying to persecute him for his vegetarian beliefs…"

Expressionless mask, expressionless mask…

"…just because he was reciting one of his poems to passers by. Just because it had the line 'Thou eaters of evil with thy carnivorous eyes' in it."

My face is now a wall.

Fax shouts from upstairs: "Can I use your Timotei m'lady?"

I stand up. "Yeah let's go to the pub." I need to do something before my face stops being a wall.

42. BRA-MAN

I'm a bit embarrassed to be going in this pub after last time. I hope the barman isn't angry with me. I'm hoping he's not even there. Maybe he's been sacked because of a disagreement about poetry.

Shit, there he is. He gives me a wave when he sees me. Oh God this means he hates me. I make Joanne and Fax go to the bar while I find a table.

It's karaoke night. A man in a t-shirt that says 'Fuck You' is singing Elvis to what I assume is his wife.

Joanne comes back with a double gin for me. "You didn't tell me what you wanted so I didn't know, and that barman started saying you really liked gin. Is that the one who brought you home the other week?"

I put my head in my hands. "Yeah that's him."

Oh God I'm never going to live that down. I was hoping he wouldn't even remember, and that he helped people home all the time. I try to sit as far down under the table as possible. I'm going to have to go apologise to him later. I'll have to make sure Joanne and Fax are busy doing something else, because I might end up having to explain what made me get hammered in the first place.

The man in the 'Fuck You' t-shirt finishes, and the

DJ gets up and launches into some spiel about how "it's party time guys and gals…" My parents would feel right at home here.

Fax goes and gets a karaoke book. Oh fucking hell no. It's one thing to have to sit there listening to him singing 'I Gave My Love A Fucking Bastard Cherry'; it's another for him to do it in the pub, in front of normal people.

They knob about over the book while I watch a lumpy woman in a boob tube singing 'Mustang Sally'. She's not bad. Oh God I'm going to have to go get another drink soon. I wonder if I can make Joanne go to the bar for me all night. I could lie on the floor doing a 'dead fish' if she says no, see how she likes it.

"OK up next we have… Fax? Is that right?"

That was quick. Joanne is screeching next to me. Fax swaggers up to the karaoke bit and does a fist pump at Joanne. Joanne won't stop going "Wooooo!" at him. The song starts up. I cringe a bit in fear before I recognise it. Well this is unexpected.

Fax has chosen Robert Palmer's 'Addicted To Love'. Against my better judgement, I don't immediately go and hide in the toilet. Fax is doing what he imagines is sexy dancing.

"The lights are on, people are bad…"

Wait, what?

"This is because they eat meat…"

Those are not the words. I look round to see people sharing my general confusion. Everyone's just sort of looking at him. Apart from Joanne, who has decided to get up and do swirly, out of time dancing. The Davina McCall moves make an appearance.

"OH! WHEN WILL THIS WAR STOP, OH YEAH!"

I think this might be a good time to get another drink. If it's between confronting the barman and having people know I'm with Fax, I'll choose the barman.

"Oh hello, are you feeling better now?"

Oh God he definitely hates me. "I'm really sorry about that," I mumble.

He laughs. "Forget it, we get a lot worse in here." He looks over at Joanne. "Is that the one you live with?"

I look down at the bar. "I live with both of them." Fuck knows what he must be thinking.

He pushes a double gin towards me. "On the house."

"Oh no you don't have to do that, they're not that bad…"

I take the gin anyway.

"I'm Aaron by the way. Not 'Bra-Man', like you were calling me last time.

My head slumps down and hits the bar. It's ashamed to be attached to me. "God I'm really sorry."

He laughs.

I pick my head up again. "If it helps, I'd just found out that the singing one had decided to move in with us while I was at work."

He looks over at Fax, who is now doing air humping. Even the man in the 'Fuck You' t-shirt looks slightly offended.

Aaron the barman nods as if this is all the explanation he needs.

"CAPITALIST HOVELS, OH YEAH!"

I down my gin.

43. ASSERTIVENESS

They've decided to become nudists for a bit. You know, just in case I'm not taking the thought of caving my own face in with the iron seriously enough.

They didn't tell me they were going to do this, I only found out when I walked into the living room yesterday morning and found Fax saluting the sun.

"Namaste!" he boomed at me. I'd only been awake 20 minutes, and wasn't entirely sure this wasn't a dream. I stood there like a fucking rabbit in some headlights, waiting for this to not be happening. As much as I tried not to look, I kept looking.

Just when my instincts were about to kick in and I was about to throw something at Fax's horrible naked bollocks, Joanne bounced into the room. Literally.

"Mel, we need to leave all the curtains and all the windows open today because we need to get as much natural light as possible."

"We're doing a cleansing," said Fax.

There was nowhere in the room I could look without seeing naked body parts. I put my hands over my eyes.

"God that's so childish" snapped Joanne. "It's perfectly natural. We've been reading a book called *Cleansing the*

Inner Soul With Spirit Light. The author channelled the Archangel Michael."

I'm pretty sure the Archangel Michael didn't tell Fax to put his bollocks in my face.

I'd gone downstairs to talk to them about a cleaning rota. We can't go on like this, no one's doing the washing up, and the hoover smells suspiciously like weed when you turn it on. It can't carry on, it's starting to be like something out of *Hoarders*. Joanne's answer to a room that needs cleaning is to put crystals in there to 'ionise' it.

I was going to put my foot down, I really was. I was going to be all assertive with them, and tell them they needed to start pulling their weight. I had it all rehearsed in my head. Everything was going to plan until I saw the... well... the Fax Machine.

"According to the channelling, man is supposed to have a period of three days every year where he eats no food but instead gets all his nutrition from sunlight," explained Joanne. "We would just go outside, but when I tried to go outside the old bitch across the road started shouting that she was going to call the police."

I have managed to avoid them since then, but tonight I am prepared. I've got bin bags, sponges and a bottle of Cillit Bang from work. I am determined. Naked or not, they are going to help me clean the house. I'm going to be assertive. I've also got some vodka for if the assertiveness doesn't go very well.

I'm glad it's dark, it means I'll probably only have to look at them by the light of the TV.

I barge into the living room to find Joanne smoking a joint and Fax knitting. *Knitting.*

I dump my bag of cleaning stuff in the middle of the floor and fix my eyes on a spot above their heads: "We are going to do some cleaning."

"We can't, we're busy."

"You are not fucking busy, you are fucking naked and annoying. This is not a discussion – I am going to do cleaning and you two are going to help me."

Fax looks up from his knitting. "I offer my services, but I cannot let m'lady do manual toil."

It's OK, I've already worked out what to do if they start making excuses. I've bought a family sized bag of dry roasted peanuts, which I take out of the carrier bag.

"Right." I open the bag, take out a peanut and throw it at Joanne.

"God what are you playing at?"

"I'm not sure how many peanuts I've got in here, but it's quite a lot. I am going to throw one peanut at you every 10 seconds until you agree to do some cleaning."

"You can't do that, that's stupid, I – ow!"

"Since Fax has already agreed to do some housework, he shall not have peanuts thrown at him. Which means I have more peanuts to throw at you."

Nevertheless, Fax is shielding himself with his knitting.

I throw another peanut. "I know you can't go outside because you're doing your stupid naked thing, so I'll just follow you round the house throwing peanuts at you. Even when you're asleep. So you might as well just agree with me now and save us both the trouble."

"Yeah well you'll run out of peanuts!"

"When I run out I'll pick them up and use them again. And then I'll be throwing second hand peanuts at you, which will be even worse."

I throw another one at her. She gets up and starts trying to dodge the peanuts.

"Stop it you mental – ow, that one hit me in the face!"

"Do some cleaning then!"

It takes 57 peanuts before she agrees to do some house-work. I know this because I count them as I pick them up.

44. PARTY

We're having this stupid party. I say 'we', really it's just me having to be in the house with those two and their circus parade of friends. Fax has joined the Tai Chi group in the park, which means they're all coming to sit in my living room, along with Spoz, scary Bonnie with the tag, and God knows who else.

At least thanks to my brilliant peanut plan, the house is now looking quite nice. Joanne and Fax, under pain of death, have moved all their shit upstairs for the time being. And they've started wearing clothes again. Words can't describe how happy I was to see Fax in his underpants, which is something I never thought I'd say.

Fax has done a tray of his 'savoury orbs' but, in a rare moment of sanity, Joanne managed to persuade him not to cook a load of eggs by holding them. He's sat fiddling with his guitar while we wait for people to arrive. Joanne is humming and sprinkling salt on the floor.

"Why are you doing that? Didn't you just hoover up?"

She rolls her eyes at me. "I'm cleansing the space, obviously!"

Of course she is. I take that as my cue to start drinking. I probably should pace myself a bit though, I'll just have some tea and vodka.

The kettle is definitely broken now. Boil beer in it once and you might get away with it, but twice turned out to be too much for it. I put a pan of tea on. Then I remember Marianne's stupid crap 'Pimms' recipe and I start laughing. I laugh so much I forget to turn the cooker on, so there is no tea, there is only a pan of water.

I turn to look at Daniel. Daniel and I have made up now; he's agreed that he was stupid and wrong to not have stopped Fax moving in, but we've agreed that there's not much we can do about it now.

"There might not be any tea Daniel."

Daniel looks at me as if to say 'You know what, you could do to lose a couple of pounds though. Why not try the Pimms?'

I stare at him. "The Pimms? Are you kidding?"

He doesn't answer. He thinks he's made his point.

"It'll still be diet Pimms if I put vodka in it, right?"

He doesn't answer.

"Right?"

He doesn't answer. I take this as a yes.

I pop to the shop for vinegar and lemonade. I don't tell those two I'm going; they'll only insist I buy nonsense. I can't forget the time I was 'popping to the shop', and Joanne asked me to buy her one of those 'magic' milk bottles for dolls where the milk disappears, and she swore she'd give me the money when I got back. She never fucking did. And I never found out what she wanted it for.

Shit, no balsamic vinegar. I don't know what makes balsamic vinegar different from normal vinegar. Probably nothing. I get a bottle of Sarsons.

When I get back Bonnie is there, along with some people I don't know. I ignore everyone and go to the kitchen.

'I can't believe you've actually fucking bought that', Daniel's look seems to say. Although I'm probably wrong. The real Daniel O'Donnell would never say 'fucking'.

They've already got a bong going. Joanne has put some music on that reminds me of Chris and the Christmas Ornament's 'Lute 'n' Flute' thing. The others apparently like it; one of them is doing what I think is Tai Chi in the middle of the room.

"Brace yourself Daniel, you're going to have lemonade and vodka and vinegar poured into you."

I make the 'diet Pimms'. It looks OK – sort of brownish. Brown is good, most booze is brown. I decide I might as well commit to the idea, so I take a big swig.

It doesn't taste like Pimms.

Then I remember that I've never actually had Pimms. Even so, I'm certain it doesn't taste of Sarsons. I spit it out into the sink.

Joanne comes in. "Oh my god are you making cocktails? Fax can do that thing where you spin the glasses round!"

I assume Fax can also melt steel with his penis.

"Let's have a try."

Before I can warn her she's grabbed Daniel and taken a huge gulp. She looks like she did when she ate the egg. Clearly I've put too much vinegar in it.

When I've stopped laughing, I take Daniel from Joanne and pour the whole lot down the sink.

"What the fuck were you making in there?"

I look at the floor. "Diet Pimms."

"Pimms?"

I look at the floor even more. "It was a Slimming World thing."

Joanne rolls her eyes. "For God's sake, are you still doing that crap? I told you, your soul knows what weight your body's supposed to be…"

I cut her off. "Yes, thank you Carol Vorderman. However, I do need to lose some weight, so I'm sticking with it. You're just skinny because you're too off your face to eat most of the time."

She stamps her foot on the floor. I thought people only did that in kids' books.

"God, I've told you already that I eat things with positive vibrations!"

"Fuck that, I've seen you eat 11 Curly Wurlys in one go!"

She doesn't reply because Bonnie comes in. I notice her tag is gone; there's a bit of her leg that's whiter than the rest.

"Where's your vodka?"

The vodka is mine. She cannot have the vodka. Joanne better not tell her I have the vodka, because then Bonnie will mug me, and I don't want that to happen.

In a massive stroke of luck, I don't think Joanne has seen my bottle of Smirnoff hiding behind the kettle. What, she thinks I just mixed lemonade and vinegar and drank it?

"We don't have any vodka Bon."

"THIS IS A CUNTING SHIT PARTY!"

One of Fax's Tai Chi people comes in. "Do you have any plasters?"

"No, sorry, what's wrong?"

"Oh, Linda kicked the TV a bit."

We go in to assess the damage. Thankfully the only thing that's injured is Linda's foot. Serve her right for having, what, size 16 feet? The stupid big cow.

Joanne and Bonnie decide they're going to go to the shop for plasters and vodka.

"Can you get some wine as well?"

Joanne looks at me. "And where's your money?"

"Can't you get it?"

All the Tai Chi people are looking at me, and they've all decided that I never buy anything in this house. Well fuck them.

"God, what, am I made of money or something?"

Fuck being polite. "Yes, yes you are! You paid for a fucking Creme Egg with a £50 note!"

"Yeah well that was, like, money I worked for. It was the vibrations!"

"So what you're saying is you won't buy me a bottle of wine, after all the stuff I've bought you."

Everyone's looking at her now. Good, because my fanny's really itchy and now I can scratch it.

"God you're such an alcoholic!"

I assume that means she's going to get some wine. Good.

Bonnie stares at the kitchen then shouts:

"ARE THOSE FUCKING SWEDISH CUPBOARDS?"

Joanne ushers her out of the room, while I stand there wondering if we have Swedish cupboards, and why they would offend someone.

I look at Daniel. "Sorry, let's just stick to vodka now."

Daniel agrees.

Spoz turns up an hour later. I wish I didn't just hate Spoz for no reason, and could be in the room with him. He has to manoeuvre to get his hair through the door. Sadly, I can't shake this feeling that he's going to stab me in the head, so I make my excuses and go stand in the kitchen.

I hear the doorbell go while I'm in the middle of a conversation with Daniel. For fuck's sake, all of Joanne's weirdo friends are here already. Who else is it going to be? Steven Seagal? NASA? Someone Bonnie threatened to kneecap once?

Joanne runs into the kitchen with… oh shit… Bra-Man. I mean, shit what was his name? Adam?

"Yo I invited Aaron!"

Aaron.

Aaron goes to shake my hand. I'm not sure why. "It's nice to be formally introduced, lol!"

He actually says 'lol', out loud.

Joanne grins at me. "I'll leave you two to get acquainted."

We stand looking at each other. I can't bring him in on the conversation I was just having with Daniel, and I can't really think of anything else to say. Evidently, neither can Aaron.

"Soooo…."

Should I clean the fridge out? It would be something to do at least.

"Soooo. You wanna dance?"

I don't 'wanna dance'. I never 'wanna dance'. And anyway, Joanne's weird music isn't the kind of music you can dance to, unless you do Tai Chi. I peer into the living room – no one's even doing the Tai Chi any more. Everyone's sitting round smoking. Bonnie is cracking her knuckles. I decide I'd rather stay in the kitchen, even if it means having Aaron the barman in it. I shake my head at Aaron.

"Soooo, your flatmate's… interesting…"

I want to tell him that she's not my fucking flatmate because we don't fucking live in a flat. The idiot. Instead I go "Ha ha, yeah."

The kitchen really fucking stinks of aftershave now. Why did Joanne invite him? And since she invited him, she should fucking be looking after him.

I hate the way Joanne just makes friends with random strangers. It always leads to trouble.

I feel guilty about being so impatient with Aaron;

after all, he did help me home that night. And he did give me a free gin. But that doesn't mean he can show up at my house and make me do small talk with him for three hours. I wish I was one of those people who didn't give a fuck, who could just go 'Well, it was nice to chat, but now I'm going to bed, nighty night!'.

But I'm not one of those people. So I stand there and listen to him talking at me, and I make words come out of my mouth in response. After a while we move to the living room, where everyone is having a shouting conversation about space travel. I bet Fax has already claimed to have been to the Moon. Everyone's shouting over everyone else, apart from Spoz, who is just sort of staring. He must have had a bad bong hit.

My mind collapses a bit then, and I realise that I really, really don't want to be at this party. I start to think of excuses to go to bed. 'I have a headache' seems to be the front runner.

Then I hear two voices simultaneously. I hear Fax shout "Kris Akabusi was really noisy in the bathroom that time he stayed over", and I hear one of the Tai Chi women shout "Naked Twister!"

"Sorry guys, I have a migraine, I'm going to have to head to bed."

45. DUEL

For once they're quiet. I mean, they're still in the room, but I'm actually able to watch *The Walking Dead*. I think they're still hungover from last night.

They're having a whispered conversation about some bollocks or other. I don't care because I'm getting better at tuning them out. I'm doing a good job of focusing on Andrew Lincoln. Andrew Lincoln makes everything better.

There's a knock at the door. I am not fucking answering it, it won't be for me. I act as if I haven't heard it. I think Joanne and Fax genuinely haven't heard it.

Another knock. "Jo, get the door, I'm watching this."

"What? Oh, yeah."

To my relief she doesn't start banging on about being 'quantumly disentangled' from Fax; she just goes to get the door. I hear a male voice. Oh for fuck's sake.

It's Spoz. He comes in and stands in front of the TV. Of course he fucking does.

"We need to have a fight. You and me. Come on."

He's talking to Fax. Fax looks startled. "Did you say you wanted to fight me?"

Spoz sniffs; it's the kind of sniff that indicates something's been up his nose that shouldn't have been. "Yeah. I want to go out with Jo, so I'll fight you for her."

Joanne stands up and throws her packet of Rizlas at him. "God we've been over this! You do not settle things by fighting for my honour!"

I have no choice but to sit and watch this unfold, since Spoz is still blocking the fucking TV.

Spoz ignores her. "You stole my woman so we have to have a fight. That's the rules."

"Oh just piss off and stop calling me your woman!"

I would join in with 'And move out of the fucking way', but I don't want him to cut me.

Fax stands up. "Fine! Fine, we'll have a duel! But I must warn you, I – OW!"

Spoz has, in my opinion, gone against the spirit of duelling for a lady's honour by kicking Fax in the bollocks. Fax jumps back just in time to avoid most of the blow, but I still think it's against the rules. At least he's moved out of the way of the TV.

Joanne starts hitting Spoz with a copy of *Spirit And Destiny*. Spoz dodges past her and starts doing weird kung fu moves at Fax. Fax responds by adopting a pose normally seen in etchings of Victorian boxers. So far this is the worst fight I've ever seen.

Joanne tries to hit Spoz again, but Fax stands in front of her and says "It's OK m'lady, this blackguard is not allowed to go out with you, because I'm going out with you."

The fight moves around the room a bit, with neither side really scoring any points. There's a bit when I think Fax is going to be able to slap Spoz in the face, but he misses.

I'm almost losing interest, but then Spoz lands a sort of punch on the side of Fax's head. This is a game changer. Fax runs into the kitchen and grabs a pan out of the sink. I'm not sure this is within the rules either, but since I'm rooting for Fax it doesn't matter. Upon seeing Fax armed with the pan, Spoz runs to the other side of the living room to plan his next move. Joanne is now keeping up a constant stream of "Pack it in you knobhead!" while, for reasons known only to her, jumping up and down on the settee.

"You're a shit in a shirt!" yells Spoz. Fax waves the pan at him. It's only the little pan; I think he'd have done better choosing the frying pan. The the two of them run round and round in a circle like this is a fucking Tom and Jerry cartoon.

I really fancy a pancake. But I know I won't bother going out to buy the stuff, and anyway by the time I get round to actually cooking, Fax might have worked out that he should be using the frying pan. I wish they'd fucking get on with this.

Fax has worked out that he needs to be close to Spoz in order to land blows on him. Unfortunately, Spoz won't stand still long enough to be hit with a pan, the selfish bastard.

This deadlock is broken when Joanne shouts "I love you Fax! Oh God you're so brave!" This declaration inspires a new vigour in Fax, and he manages to twat Spoz on the arm with the pan. Spoz runs into the kitchen. Fax runs in after him. Half a second later, there's a crashing sound, followed by a smash. For a split second I wonder if Fax has knocked over some cans of pop, then I remember that we don't have a shelf full of pop in our kitchen. I wish we did.

We run into the kitchen and find Spoz lying on the floor. He's alive, but I still don't like him. Fax is brandishing the pan in victory.

"Ha!"

He says something to Joanne, but I'm not listening because I've just seen what caused the smashing sound. On the floor, next to the recycling that I'm always meaning to take out, Daniel is lying in a million pieces.

I don't move. I don't hear Joanne cheering at Fax's victory. I don't notice Spoz scuttling away calling Fax a bellend.

My brain is telling me to calm down, that it might not be Daniel, that it might be some other mug. But I know it's Daniel, because I can see one of his eyes looking at me.

It's about a year before Joanne and Fax stop singing 'We Are the Champions'. They come into the kitchen to see why I'm not celebrating with them. They look where I'm looking, and when it finally twigs Joanne claps her hand over her mouth like she's in a sodding TV movie.

"Oh God..."

I tear my eyes away from Daniel. "Yes it is oh God."

My overwhelming emotion is guilt. I had a go at Daniel, and now he's dead. I blamed him for letting Fax move in, when it was me who should have put my foot down and stopped the weird bastard moving in. And now the weird bastard has killed Daniel.

My guilt quickly turns to rage. I spin round to face the hairy fucking fop:

"YOU DID THIS!"

Then I add:

"YOU HAIRY FUCKING FOP!"

Joanne leaps to his defence. Of course she fucking does. She only cares about Fax; fuck the fact that I am now a fucking widow, and that she's choosing a fucking murderer over her best friend.

"He didn't do it! Spoz fell on him, the twat!"

I notice Fax is now hiding behind Joanne. To be fair, he has good reason to hide behind Joanne, because I am going to murder him.

46. GOOD NEWS

The phone wakes me up. I open one eye and hope it's an assassin who's somehow found my number and is offering to come round and kill Joanne and Fax, preferably for less than three quid.

Shit went down last night. It really did. I don't remember all of it, but I do remember the following:

1. Me chasing Fax round the house with the frying pan
2. Me threatening to report Fax to NASA (can't remember why)
3. Me trying to phone a funeral parlour about Daniel (thank God they were shut)
4. Joanne buying me a bottle of gin as a bribe, which ended up causing number 3

It's Karen on the phone. For a second I panic and wonder if I'm supposed to be at work. Have I done something ridiculous like sleep for a week?

"Mel? Hi, it's Karen! Guess what?"

I've always wondered about this. When people say 'guess what', do they really want you to try and guess? Because it would take people a fucking long time. It could be something to do with the Pyramids, or it could be that they've got a song stuck in their head. I'm not sure Karen would phone me because she has a song stuck in her head though.

"What?"

"I'm having a baby!"

Oh wow. I sit up in bed and pay attention. Karen has finally managed to make her ovaries listen to her. This is nice news; I find myself smiling, which is something my face isn't really used to at the moment.

"Wow that's brilliant!"

She does a squeak. "I've wanted to tell you for a while now, but I didn't want to jinx it until I knew everything was OK. He's due around January!"

Ooh, Jeremy then. I should buy him something. Maybe a briefcase?

We carry on making woman noises for a bit, and then Karen says:

"The other thing is, do you remember I said I'd be leaving to have my baby? So there's going to be a manager's job if you want it."

I vaguely remember her nagging me about something; she might have mentioned leaving.

"Why don't you come into the shop and I'll take you through everything?"

Well I guess I'm going to be the manager of the Co-op whether I like it or not. I can't think of a good reason to refuse this offer. What could I say? 'Oh no thank you I'd rather not have a slightly better paid job if you don't mind'? It doesn't look that hard anyway; Karen just sits about in the back mostly.

When I get to the shop we do some more squeaky woman noises, and Karen launches into a monologue about 'breast feeding Jeremy' and 'lemon paint for the nursery'. Then we have a cup of tea and Karen serves a couple of people. After this, instead of her showing me the manager stuff, I find myself telling her about Joanne and Fax, about them going round naked, about their loud sex and Joanne's weird scary friends, and about Daniel. I go on for longer than I mean to.

Karen hands me a Kit Kat. "You've got to move out. You'll be getting an extra four grand a year, you can easily get your own place."

I find myself instinctively defending Joanne, but when I try to do this I can't make the words come out of my mouth.

"I mean, can you imagine living like this for the rest of your life?"

I shrug. It's hard to tell her to fuck off in my head when I know she's right.

"You know I've never liked her, that's no secret. She's a deadbeat, and now she's got her friends coming round and breaking all your stuff? You're not seriously telling me you're going to put up with her behaviour forever? I mean, can you imagine getting to 35, or even 40, and still living with her and that weirdo boyfriend?"

I get a vision of a 70 year old me, walking through the house on my Zimmer frame. Joanne and Fax are still going round having sex and being naked, but now it's even worse because they're elderly and Joanne's tits drag on the floor.

And anyway, if I'm honest with myself, I reached the same conclusion as Karen last night, when I saw Daniel lying on the floor. I knew then that I would have to do something, that I couldn't carry on doing this. I decided that this would end one of two ways – either I would move out, or I would kill the pair of them. Since I already tried to murder Fax last night, and it didn't go very well, I guess I'm stuck with the first option.

I sigh and eat my Kit Kat.

47. ANNOUNCEMENT

It's been a week since my talk with Karen. I've been busy.

I didn't go straight home after I left the shop, I went and sat in the park and thought about my life. I came to the conclusion that my life seems to consist mainly of being pissed, staring into space, and being annoyed with Joanne.

I wondered if I could ever be one of those people you see in magazines. You know, the people who have stuff that they do. And they have things like a long jar for spaghetti, and some friends that they can stand to be around. They do things like, I dunno, roller skating.

After a while, my legs tried to make me stand up to go home, but my brain kept stopping them. The thought of what I might find those two doing stopped me moving. It wouldn't surprise me at all to find they've built a bonfire in the living room and are dancing around it while eating Smarties. It also occurred to me that I now know all the words to 'I Gave My Love A Cherry'.

There were some people having a bit of a picnic not far from me. They looked nice and normal. They were drinking pink wine and eating sausage rolls and stuff. They weren't swigging from a bottle of ouzo and eating savoury orbs.

As I looked at them, what I wanted more than anything was to swap lives with them, just for a bit, just to see what it was like. I sat and stared at them, and eventually my brain piped up with 'Well, no one's going to do it for you. If you want to be those people you'll have to get your shit together'.

So I did.

I became all determined, like those sassy ladies you see on Jerry Springer. I marched home and went straight online. Turns out there are loads of cheap flats if you actually look for them. I picked one that looked nice, and I phoned the landlord. I hovered over my mobile for five minutes before I actually made the phone call. I started arguing with myself.

'Are you really sure you want to do this?'

'Really? Moving out? You don't even have any boxes.'

'What if there's a burglar and you can't use Joanne and Fax as human shields?'

Then my eyes fell on the shoe box in the corner of the room. Daniel's remains live in there now. I'd thought about burying him, but I don't like to think about a dog coming along and doing a wee on that bit of ground. Anyway, we don't have a garden and I'm probably not allowed to bury him in the park.

How many more Daniels were there going to be? How much more of my stuff was she going to break, or piss in, or have sex near?

What made me finally make the phone call was the certainty that, for as long as I was living with Joanne and Fax, I was never going to have a long spaghetti jar.

The landlord wanted someone to move in as soon as possible. The next day, when I'd been to see the place and met the landlord and sorted everything out, I went into the living room and turned the TV off. Joanne and Fax had been watching some alien conspiracy shit.

"I'm moving out."

It took them a while to register what I said. Then they both gawped at me. Joanne piped up:

"Why?"

I dithered over whether to be honest or not. Should I say 'Well actually, it's because I cannot stand to be around you and your stupid Edwardian boyfriend for another second. I had about 1% patience with you when it was just the two of us, but your constant musical sex and general dicking about has now made my life unbearable'? I went with this.

This was the wrong thing to say, because Joanne started crying. Then Fax started crying because Joanne was crying. Then Fax ran upstairs, still crying.

Joanne rugby tackled my legs, which made me fall over.

"Don't leave!"

I wasn't expecting this. If anything, I was expecting them to be quite pleased, given that my moving out meant they could have sex all over the house without me shouting at them.

"jkvhiurvofiucfsefi!"

Oh God not this again. I stood back up. "Look, it's for the best."

"ouefocjgyf!!!!"

"Yes but I'm still moving out."

This went on for about 10 minutes, and then Fax came back into the room waving a piece of paper:

"I've written you a poem…"

A poem? Oh for fuck's sake, if there's anything about my feet in it…

He got down on one knee and cleared his throat.

"This is called 'M'Lady's Handmaiden'":

"Oh, thou art a bit fat but lovely of face,

And thy maketh m'lady full of good cheer,
Also, thou do the shopping, don't go!…"

Before he could go on I kicked him over. Joanne slapped me on the arm, then immediately went back to hugging my legs.

When I finally managed to untangle Joanne, and when Fax had stopped crying again, I resumed my speech.

"This is not working out. I do not want poems written for me that are vaguely insulting anyway, and I'm sick of you pissing in my things!"

I looked at Joanne. Fax looked at Joanne. Clearly she'd never told him this anecdote.

"God, it was only once!"

"I – look." I put my head in my hands. "Look, I'm going. I've made my mind up. I've already put down a deposit."

Joanne had one last attempt at persuading me to stay by doing her 'dead fish', but it wasn't going to sway me.

All the shit poetry in the world can't compete with having a long spaghetti jar and not hearing those two have sex all the time. Plus, it's what Daniel would have wanted.

48. THE LIST

My new flat is lovely. It's all magnolia. That's a nice normal colour. For months I've had to put up with a bright yellow living room because Joanne claimed yellow 'went well with the moon' or some such bullshit. Just looking at it burned my retinas.

Well, fuck Joanne. Let her have her stupid highlighter pen living room. I don't have to do any of that bollocks any more. I'm still excited by the novelty of the place; sometimes I just wander round, listening to how quiet it is, and enjoying the fact that there are no crystals or tarot cards anywhere.

I don't have my long spaghetti jar yet, but I'm definitely getting to that. Last night, after I watched *The Walking Dead* with no interruptions, I wrote a list. This is my list:

1. Lose weight. (As in, actually start taking Slimming World seriously and not just going there to get stickers and laugh at people.)
2. Buy a long spaghetti jar
3. Do some socializing with some people who aren't mental hippies
4. Maybe get some sort of boyfriend
5. Open that 'Learn French in a week' thing my mum

bought me last year

I've made a good start to my new life by moving into this flat. It's the sort of flat that normal people have. The only thing in here that I might have trouble explaining is the shoebox full of Daniel bits, which is on a shelf with some candles. It's definitely not a shrine. I might get a photo of Daniel O'Donnell to go on it though.

When I get my long spaghetti jar, I will invite my friends round for spaghetti. When I get some new friends. Anyway, they'll come round for spaghetti, and we'll all eat spaghetti and sauce that I've made myself, and we'll talk about things like TV shows and politics, instead of talking about the Archangel Michael and Fax's penis.

49. CARROT STICKS, PART 3

This week I am Marianne's star pupil. I've lost another two-and-a-half-pounds. This is great, because it means I'm sticking to number 1 on the list. I'm not slimmer of the week though, because Mandy has lost four pounds, and now she's technically not supermorbidly obese any more. We all clap.

Slimmer of the week doesn't matter that much right now anyway. It's the losing weight that counts. If I keep this up, I should be down to a size 12 soon. This is great.

We all sit round on our chairs. Already I feel like my bum fits in the chair more comfortably. Marianne starts talking about this week's subject, and for once I'm not fighting the urge to boo her. I've decided I'm going to listen to what she says, and actually try to do it. If I'm serious about my list I need to commit properly.

"Right ladies! Since we're moving into autumn, it's time to think about hearty comfort food for when the nights start drawing in!"

Comfort food. I like comfort food. The old me would class 20 chicken nuggets and some sambuca as comfort food, but the new me is going to try something different.

Marianne holds up a picture of an egg in a baking tray.

"Now then ladies! Egg and chips is a go-to comforting meal for many of us, and I'm happy to say you can still have this! Simply fry one egg in Fry Light or a similar one calorie spray, and serve with up to eight chips! And this is a completely free and warming Slimming World winter meal!"

I never thought I'd hear the phrase 'up to eight chips' in my life.

But maybe she's got a point. I mean, who needs all those chips anyway? Surely I can learn to be full after eight chips? I mean, it's what thin people do. People in magazines.

Then Marianne reels off a recipe for something called 'Cheesy broccoli one pot bake', but instead of cheese you're supposed to use something called 'quark', which I've never heard of. I must look that up. I think I've seen it in *Star Trek*.

Then she holds up a picture of what she claims is a pizza. It doesn't look like a pizza. For a start I can't see any dough; it just looks like a plate of tomato stuff. But maybe this is what I'm supposed to be doing? Maybe only really fat people eat pizza. The new me can't eat pizza. I'm determined.

After class I pop to Tesco to get some bits. I'd meant to write down the Slimming World recipes, but I forgot to bring a pen and now I can't really remember anything. I know that fruit and veg is always a good thing to have on Slimming World. I stop at the fruit and veg bit.

There are some bags of carrot sticks. I wonder if I should buy one. I don't really like carrots, but Marianne is always going on about them, and look how thin she is. I should try to be more like Marianne. I put the carrot sticks into my basket.

Then I get some diet coke and some eggs. And this time

I'll cook the eggs properly rather than letting Fax try to magic them. For fuck's sake.

When I get home, I put the TV on, pour myself a glass of diet coke and open the bag of carrot sticks. I have a nibble of one. It's not too bad. It's not something I'd necessarily choose to eat, but they're really good for you, so I'll have a few more.

50. FUN

I've been ordered to go out with some of the 'ladies' from Slimming World. It's someone's birthday, I don't know. The old me wouldn't have gone, but the new me has to do things like this, because it's what people in magazines do. They go out with 'the girls', and they drink cocktails and wave their arms around. So far we haven't waved our arms around, but I'm sure that part's coming. Plus, this is number 3 on the list.

There are ten of us; I'd estimate that we've got a combined weight of 300 stone. We're all sitting round a big table in one of those chain pubs, I don't remember the name of it. So far I've grinned approximately 97 times, although nothing's really been that funny.

One of the fat women is telling us an anecdote about a holiday in Majorca. I think that's what it's about, it's hard to tell over the music. But I assume it's hilarious because the other women are screeching. I screech along with them. This is great.

Some of us are sharing a jug of mojito. I'd expected it to be a bit stronger than it is, I guess it's been watered down by all the ice. It tastes like pop. I had expected to be more pissed than this by now. But it's good because I should stop drinking so much anyway. There are loads of 'syns' in booze.

The music changes, and one of the medium sized women stands up and announces that she's going to go dance. This is brilliant, this is where we start waving our arms around.

It's been a long time since I've danced. I think the last time I did any proper dancing was when I was 17, and I accidentally damaged a man's top. But it's OK now because I'm not dancing with a lit cigarette.

Five of us move over to the dancefloor. There are two guys dancing already – one of them is wearing a sweat-shirt with a medallion over it. I don't put my fist in my mouth, I just laugh, but it's OK because I'm pointing my face away from him so it just looks like I'm having lots of fun. Which I am.

Dancing is quite hard. I'm getting tired halfway through the first song, and I can't figure out how to make my hips move in time with my feet, or where to put my feet. I think I just need to practice. It would help if a song I liked came on, but they're not likely to start playing Motorhead, so I guess I'll just have to work with this.

Then I have an idea. I saw a music video a few months ago, and the woman in it was doing a sort of crouching, arse-shaking move. So I decide to do that. Unfortunately, Medallion Man is now dancing right behind me, only I didn't realise this because I turned away so I could laugh at him. My arse knocks into him, and he spills his drink.

I turn round expecting a tirade of 'Move it you stupid fat bitch!', but all I get is him laughing and a thumbs up. This is great.

I do some more dancing, and when the next song comes on I decide to do some arm waving, then I can tick that off the list. Actually, I'm not sure it's on the list, but

I have to do it anyway.

I wave my arms around. This isn't as fun as they make it look in magazines. My arms get tired after 30 seconds. So does the rest of my body, so I decide to go get another drink. There's plenty of time for dancing later.

I'm waiting for my double vodka when I feel someone poke me:

"Hiya!"

I turn round. It's Bra-Man. Oh shit, what's his name? Oh, Aaron. I briefly wonder why he's here, since this isn't his pub. Then I work out that it's probably his night off.

He offers to pay for my drink. It would be rude not to accept, but then I have to tell him that I'm technically on a 'girls' night out'. He doesn't see a problem with joining us.

"But what about your friends?"

I look round and see a group of men cheering at Aaron. Those are his friends then. Oh sod it, he might as well come and sit with us. It's all the same to me.

We head back to my table, where the women who aren't dancing immediately crowd round Aaron. Some of them want to mother him, some of them want to have sex with him. I want another drink. I finished my double vodka while I wasn't looking. That was sneaky of me. I'd better get something bigger this time. I head back to the bar. Aaron follows me.

"Soooo, are you celebrating?"

No I'm really fucking not. But then I remember the new me, and I plaster a grin on my face.

"Yes, it's a birthday night out."

"Cool. Soooo, can I buy you another drink?"

I don't really want him to buy me another drink, because that would mean I'm limited to what I can get, and what I really want is ten gins. Could I push my luck and ask him to buy me ten gins? Probably not.

"No it's OK thanks, I'm getting quite a lot, so…"

"Oh are you getting drinks for your friends? OK no worries."

Maybe ten gins is a bit excessive. I get four, and Aaron stands there and lets me pay for them. He makes conversation with me while he's waiting for his pint –

"Soooo, how's your flatmate?"

Instead of punching him I say "Oh, she's not my flatmate any more. I moved out."

"Oh no, why?"

Why did he assume it's bad that I've moved out? He's met Joanne.

"It was just a bit crowded and, you know…"

"Oh, yeah."

We give up on conversation. Aaron gets his pint then follows me back to my table. I wonder if his friends are pissed off with him for abandoning them, but they can probably survive without him going 'Soooo'.

Nothing much happens for a bit, and then I go to the toilet. One of the Slimming World women comes with me. I think her name's Kath but I can't really remember. That'll do anyway.

Kath lurks behind me while I'm staring into the mirror. "Is that your boyfriend?"

It takes me a second to work out she's talking about Aaron. "Oh, no, he's just someone I know."

"Oh, well he wants to be. You should go out with him love, you two would make a lovely couple."

I don't think we would. I get a mental image of Aaron looming over me while singing 'I Gave My Love A Cherry'.

"I've seen him looking at you like a poor lost puppy. You should grab him while you can!"

Then she leaves, in fits of giggles. After a few minutes I realise that she might have been implying I'm old and desperate, but I don't think she was because she's in her fifties.

An hour later, the gin has done its work. I'm pissed enough to have another go at dancing, and I've stopped caring that I can't really hear what any of them are saying.

Aaron is dancing next to me. He's better at it than I am. He seriously needs to lay off the aftershave though.

"Soooo, can I have your number then?"

For a second my mental brain thinks he means my PIN number, and then I realise he means my phone number. I stop dancing.

"What for?"

"Well, I thought I could take you out for a meal or something…"

"Oh…"

I weigh this up in my head. On one hand I don't really fancy Aaron. I mean, he's good looking if you like that sort of thing I suppose, but the pink shirt and the aftershave don't really do it for me. On the other hand, the new me is determined to be open to new experiences, and to go out on dates and stuff. I give him my number. Then I look over at my table and see that the woman called Kath is giving me a thumbs up.

51. BRA-MAN, PART 2

Aaron and I are sitting at the table, waiting for our food. I didn't get a starter because I'm really watching my 'syns' now, and anyway we're paying for our own meals apparently.

I'm having the scampi, and Aaron is having… something. I sort of zoned out when he was ordering.

Aaron has tried several times to come out with 'conversation starters' – you know, those questions that you're supposed to ask on a date to break the ice. I read about them once.

This is the most sober date I've ever been on. So far I've only had one glass of white wine, and white wine might as well not count as booze. Normally on a date we'd both be hammered and snogging by now, but maybe I'm a bit old to be doing all that. I haven't been on a date for a couple of years. I should probably just go with this.

"Sooo, if you were a tree, which tree would you be?"

I don't fucking know, a fucking dead one. I squint at Aaron and try to pretend he's Andrew Lincoln.

I shrug at Aaron/Andrew:

"Erm, I don't know."

Then we sit in silence for a bit. Clearly he's run out of ice breakers. That aftershave is going to put me off my scampi.

Eventually Aaron breaks the silence. "Sooo."

I'm getting a bit annoyed with myself. The new me should be making more of an effort. I try to smile, and say:

"I guess I'd be a Christmas Tree, because I like Christmas."

He snorts at this. "I mean, Christmas is OK, but it's a bit commercial these days. Like Valentine's Day…"

I drift into a vision of a future Valentine's Day where I'm somehow going out with Aaron. Instead of giving me a card and some chocolates, he hands me an empty box and says 'Valentine's Day is a scam. I took the money I would have bought your present with and used it to buy some more aftershave. I'm running low on aftershave…'

The new me is screaming at the old me that I should stop being a cow and give him a chance. The old me replies with 'I really want a drink'.

Now Aaron is in the middle of a monologue about his degree. Oh, I see, he's working as a barman because he's doing a degree.

"I'm doing a module called 'Diversity and Inclusive Practice with Women'. The tutorials are OK, but I think they could be more challenging."

He waits for my reaction, and his medal.

I nod. Where's my scampi?

"What I'm really looking forward to is next year's 'Suspect populations and insecure spaces'."

I nod again.

Our food arrives. Aaron's ordered a burger that's so big it has a stick in it to hold it together. He picks up his knife and fork.

"Wait, are you going to eat that with a knife and fork?"

"Well, yeah, duh! Lol."

I've never met anyone who says 'lol', out loud.

To counter this, I start eating my scampi with my hands. Aaron gives me a look.

"What?"

"They have, you know, cutlery! Lol!"

Oh my god. I start thinking about the possibility of injecting vodka into my scampi. I could probably do it, if I had a syringe, but I don't think this place does syringes.

Him eating a burger with a knife and fork is pissing me off more than it should, but I try to ignore it. The new me would ignore it.

As we eat we try to talk about music, but Aaron says he likes something called 'dubstep' and I'm not sure I know what that is. It sounds suspiciously like that thumping music that people play in their cars late at night.

"I'm more of a rock person. I like Metallica and stuff like that. You know, something with a tune…"

He snorts. "Oh God I can't stand all that greasy moshpit stuff."

I finish my scampi.

We don't have a pudding because Aaron points out that "Aren't you doing Slimming World?" I agree that I am, and we pay the bill. As we're walking out, Aaron suggests "going into town".

"No, I think I'm a bit tired, sorry."

"Oh, OK."

Then he lunges at me with his mouth. Shit. I sort of manage to dodge him so he ends up kissing my ear. My ear will probably smell of aftershave for a week now.

"Oh sorry, I just thought…"

I look at the floor. "Yeah, maybe it's not such a good idea. I mean, you're a nice guy and stuff, but, you know…"

"…What?"

"Well, you know, maybe we don't have that much in common, and maybe this isn't a good idea."

And you're fucking annoying and you use too much cutlery and you stink of aftershave and I have no idea what you're supposed to be studying at university.

He puts his hands in his pockets. "Oh right, OK."

"Well, nighty night then, See you around."

"Yeah."

I start walking home. Aaron walks in the opposite direction.

On my way home I analyse the night. It could have gone better, but it could have gone worse. The old me wouldn't have even gone on a date with Aaron in the first place. At least I'm open to new experiences now. This is a great start.

52. FUN, PART 2

I've decided to tackle number 5 on the list, so now I'm sitting on my settee with a nice cup of green tea (apparently it's good for your metabolism). I'm leafing through the 'Learn French in a week' introductory booklet. All I can think about is that, if I'd learned French before, I wouldn't have had that trouble with my phone going all in French, and having to take it to the man to get it put back to English. That was really embarrassing.

This is going to be great though. Maybe when I'm done with this I'll do a night class or something. I could do painting, or creative writing. Maybe I'll even do a degree, although I'm not sure what I'd want to do. Not that thing Aaron was talking about.

Before any of that, though, I'm going to become fluent in French. People in magazines speak more than one language; you see them sitting at tables in pavement cafes in Europe, and they order things from the menu in foreign. I'm sure they do. Plus, when I meet a nice guy and go on a date with him, he's bound to be impressed when I start speaking French at him.

I mean, I know the date with Aaron didn't go very well, but it was definitely the right thing to do, because that's what people do. They go out on dates. I'm going to go on more dates. Just not with Aaron.

Right, page one: 'Greetings and introductions'. How do you pronounce this word? I wish I'd paid attention at school. Oh I know, I'll put the CD on. In fact, I can probably just learn the whole thing from the CD. That's what people do isn't it? They learn languages by being immersed in the language.

I'm quite tired. Oh, it's only eight o'clock. I'd better not stay up too late.

You know what would really get me in the mood for learning French? Some red wine. There isn't a shop round here, but I could nip into work and get a bottle. I can do that now I'm the boss.

Maybe later. When I've learnt some words.

Right: *Bonjour*. I already know that, it means Hello. I feel smug to be so far ahead. This is going to be a piece of piss. *Oui*. I know that one too! This is fantastic. I'm going to be fluent in an hour.

Hmm. *Comment est-ce que vous vous appelez?* What's that? I don't know that one. I flick through the book to see what it is, but the man's already moved onto *D'où êtes-vous?*. Shit. I stop the CD. You know what, a bottle of wine will relax me and make learning easier. It's fine because I can use my 'flexible syns' for it. All I have to do is not have any bad food tomorrow.

I try again when I get back from the Co-op. I got two bottles, just in case. I mean, not that I'm going to drink both of them or anything. This time I put the CD player next to me, so I can pause it when I need to.

Right, that first one means 'What is your name?' Fine, got that. I listen to it a couple of times, and before I know it my wine glass is empty. I didn't mean to do that. It must be that I'm getting engrossed in French culture.

I pause the CD, and my mind drifts off into visions of the future dinner/spaghetti parties I'll be having. I'll be able to do things like make jokes in French, and everyone will laugh, also in French. I'll be really thin by then, and everyone will be really impressed when I present my spaghetti with my homemade sauce.

I glance at the clock. Somehow an hour has gone by, and now my second glass is empty. You know what, maybe I shouldn't try to run before I can walk. Maybe I should put the French away for the evening. I mean, I'd hate to rush with the learning and end up missing bits out. I'll come back to it after work tomorrow. That's the sensible thing to do.

I put the TV on. QVC are selling a vibrating plate thing that promises to tone your arms. It looks quite good, but I probably won't get one. I watch the presenter trying not to mess up his suit as he vibrates, and I finish my wine.

53. PRESENT

There's a knock at the door. I run through the possibilities in my head:

1. Jehovah's Witnesses
2. Andrew Lincoln's car has broken down
3. One of the 'girls' has come round for a 'nice chat'
4. I hope it's not Aaron

None of these possibilities sounds any good apart from number 2. While the likelihood of number 2 being correct is slim, it's enough of a possibility to make me get up and answer the door.

"Yo."

Oh for fuck's sake. Although I'm impressed she's managed to prise herself away from Fax for a bit.

"Can I come in or what?"

"I don't know, I've got a magnolia flat, so…"

"…"

"…"

"Oh, I got you a present."

She hands me an Amazon box. It could contain anything from envelopes to a live dog. Although it would have to be quite a small dog. And also probably dead.

I'd only given her my new address so she could forward

my mail. I'm not sure why I bothered; she'd probably just roll my mail up and try to smoke it. Still, she's here now, I should probably let her come in for a bit.

She walks into the living room. The living room starts to smell of patchouli before she's even been here a minute.

"If you ask me, this place is really badly aligned, spiritually speaking."

"I didn't ask you."

"Don't be like that. Look –" She pulls a bottle of vodka out of her bag. "I got this. Do you have any cups?"

I'm still holding the Amazon box. I put it on the settee. "I have proper glasses now."

"Wow." She looks genuinely impressed.

"Fax not with you?"

"No, he's at Tai Chi." she goes over to inspect my Daniel shrine. "He's really upset that you didn't like his poem."

"He called me fat in it!"

"No he didn't, not properly. Anyway, shall we have a drink?"

Against my better judgement, I go into the kitchen and get two glasses. When I come back she's put the Amazon box on the floor and she's sprawled out on the settee. On my settee.

"Can you sit up please?"

"Well I could do but I have a bad back, because me and Fax found this rowan tree the other day…"

I don't press her for details. I busy myself with pouring the drinks.

"Are you going to open your present?"

I eye the box. "What is it?"

"God, open it and see!"

I have a big gulp of vodka, just to be polite. Then I tackle the box. My money's on something like a necklace featuring the face of Tony Blair or something equally mental. Mind you, the box might be a bit big for that. Oh Jesus, I bet it's some fucking crystals.

I open the box. It's –

Oh my god.

It's an Andrew Lincoln mug. Andrew Lincoln's lovely, zombie-killing face is gazing out at me from a mug.

I can't speak for a minute. She's actually got me something good.

"I had it made specially. There's a place and they put photos on mugs."

I look at her. I look at Andrew.

"It's brilliant."

"Yeah, I thought I'd make up for your other one. Sorry and all that."

I must christen Andrew immediately. I pour quite a lot of vodka into him. Then I refill Joanne's glass.

"Thank you."

"You're welcome. Fax paid for half of it, because he's set up his own vibrational awareness online course. He was born to be a teacher of others."

I have a swig out of Andrew. Part of me feels a bit guilty, what with Daniel's remains being in the room, but I guess you have to move on eventually.

Joanne empties her glass. "So what have you been up to?"

I find myself telling her about the dancing, and the date with Aaron. I don't mention the carrot sticks.

Then she starts telling me about Bonnie getting arrested for shouting at a woman in Matalan and accusing her of being Russian. Before I know it I'm lying on the floor giggling.

I top up our drinks. Maybe I should get some more in, this is probably going to be a late night.